"I haven't slept a wink for thinking of you, Jane," he said, and lowered his head to kiss her.

Jane's heart trembled in tune with her lips. When he firmed her lips with his kiss, her heart trembled the harder and her knees turned to water. The warmth of his body seeped into hers in a thrilling intimacy she had never even imagined, disarming her hostility. His arms tightened insensibly until he was crushing her against the hard wall of his masculinity. It was like a dream, washing away all the doubts and fears and anger that had engulfed her. He had missed her! He must care for her, at least a little. For a full minute she succumbed to the madness, before sanity returned. . . .

By Joan Smith
Published by Fawcett Books:

THE SAVAGE LORD GRIFFIN
GATHER YE ROSEBUDS
AUTUMN LOVES: An Anthology
THE GREAT CHRISTMAS BALL
NO PLACE FOR A LADY
NEVER LET ME GO
REGENCY MASQUERADE
THE KISSING BOUGH
A REGENCY CHRISTMAS: An Anthology
DAMSEL IN DISTRESS
A KISS IN THE DARK
THE VIRGIN AND THE UNICORN
A TALL DARK STRANGER
TEA AND SCANDAL

TEA AND SCANDAL

Joan Smith

FAWCETT CREST • NEW YORK

A Fawcett Crest Book
Published by Ballantine Books
Copyright © 1996 by Joan Smith

All rights reserved under International and Pan-American Copyright Conventions. Published in the United States by Ballantine Books, a division of Random House, Inc., New York, and simultaneously in Canada by Random House of Canada Limited, Toronto.

http://www.randomhouse.com

Library of Congress Catalog Card Number: 95-96158

ISBN 0-449-22492-9

Manufactured in the United States of America

First Edition: June 1996

10 9 8 7 6 5 4 3 2 1

Chapter One

Jane Lonsdale leaned back against the velvet squabs of a well-sprung carriage and gazed out at the passing countryside. It was an unaccustomed luxury for her to be traveling in a private carriage. On the other occasion she had visited her aunt Fay at Wildercliffe, she had traveled on the stage. At that time, her aunt had been Lady Pargeter's hired companion. Lady Pargeter had died since then. Fay was fortunate that Lord Pargeter had asked her to remain on as his housekeeper. As a working lady herself, Jane was intimately aware of the difficulty of finding a good position.

It was the circumstance of Jane's taking a position at Miss Prism's Academy for Young Ladies at Bath that had caused that former visit. As Jane had nowhere to go for Christmas, Fay had invited her to Wildercliffe, in the Cotswold Hills, less than a day's drive away.

What would Aunt Fay think when she landed in with two trunks holding the sum total of her worldly possessions? Worse, what would Lord Pargeter think? He was a very toplofty gentleman. Aunt Fay's letter could hardly have arrived more opportunely—on the very day Miss Prism turned her off. Jane's cheeks flushed in shame to remember the dreadful moment when she had been caught in Mr. Fortini's arms—and in a classroom, too, where a student might have come barging in at any moment.

Mr. Fortini was a passionate Italian. He had attacked her, but try telling Miss Prism that. Fortini, the visiting music master, was nothing but a lecher. He pestered all the female teachers. But Miss Prism had a tendre for him, and so it was the innocent victim who was punished by dismissal.

Jane glanced at her watch—4:00 P.M. She should be at Wildercliffe within the hour. She gazed out at the passing scene. Limestone cottages nestled against the hillside, as if seeking shelter from the wind. It seemed everything was built of stone here in Cotswold country. Sheep dotted the fields, their lambs frolicking amongst them in this spring season. Silver streams flowed through the meadows. The idyllic surroundings took the sharp edge from Jane's anxiety, but a heavy burden rested on her heart. It would be extremely difficult to find another position without a character reference from Miss Prism.

Forty-five minutes later, the carriage passed through the picturesque village of Bibury. Soon they left the main road and entered the park of Wildercliffe. This was Jane's second visit, but she was surprised anew by the beauty and grandeur of the estate. Tantalizing glimpses of gray stone were visible through the scattered trees. Then the carriage turned the corner, and the house rose before her in all its splendor. It stood three stories high, with a row of statues along the roofline. On either end a lower wing extended, curving gracefully toward the rear. The pedimented doorway was fronted by a set of broad steps. Stone urns topped the stone banister posts.

The groom pulled up to the front of the house and opened the carriage door.

"I shall go around to the rear with you and enter by the kitchen," Jane said. That high stickler Lord Pargeter would not like his housekeeper's guest to use the main entrance.

"Lady Pargeter particularly said I should bring you to the front door, madam," the groom said.

"Lady Pargeter!" It seemed his lordship had remarried. Fay had not mentioned it in her letter. He had not waited long! His first wife had only been dead eight months. The new wife sounded an extremely obliging lady, allowing her housekeeper's guest to use the front door!

Jane mounted the broad staircase. Before she could knock, the carved oaken door was opened by the stiff-faced butler.

"Welcome to Wildercliffe, Miss Lonsdale," Broome said, and ushered her in. "I shall announce you."

Jane said, "Oh, that is not necessary, Broome. If you will just take me to Miss Rampling's quarters, I believe she is expecting me." She felt uneasy in the baroque magnificence of a pink marbled floor spreading around her like a gleaming pond, and a massive chandelier hanging overhead.

The smile that twisted Broome's lips looked far from at home there. He bowed and walked to the wide doorway that pierced the wall on the left. It gave a glimpse of the long Blue Saloon beyond. Corners of marble fireplaces, gilt-framed pictures, and sofas were to be seen, but not Lady Pargeter.

"Miss Lonsdale has arrived, your ladyship," he announced.

Jane wished she could hide behind the six-foot Chinese vase in the corner, or turn to marble like the statues in the hall. She mentally prepared her apologies. "Some misunderstanding, your ladyship—"

"Well, show her in, Broome," a haughty voice said. The voice sounded vaguely familiar, yet Jane knew no one who spoke with such self-consequence except Miss Prism, and certainly Miss Prism was not Lady Pargeter.

Broome ushered Jane in. Her eyes turned to the chaise longue by the grate, where a well-padded lady of a certain age, dressed in a deep blue velvet gown with a trailing skirt, reclined at her ease. Her blond hair was arranged in a crown of curls. At her wrist, a sapphire and diamond bracelet twinkled.

"Come and give your old auntie a kiss, Jane," she said.

"Aunt Fay?" Jane said, staring in bewilderment.

"You can call me Lady Pargeter. I married him."

For a full thirty seconds, Jane was speechless. Fay had always been a great jokesmith, but this was going too far. Lord Pargeter might appear at any moment, and with his hot temper, he would send them both packing.

"Come and have a seat, dear," Fay said, sitting up and patting the chaise longue. "You look like a ghost."

Jane managed to make it to the chaise longue. Fay handed her a glass of wine, saying, "Drink this down. It'll put the roses back in your cheeks. I didn't mean to give you a turn. I should have told you. I was saving it for a surprise."

"But it cannot be true. Lord Pargeter married to

4

you? He always called you Rampling in that odious way and treated you like a servant."

"That was before Lizzie died. His grief softened him up."

"Lady Pargeter has only been dead eight months."

"Aye, we did rush it somewhat, but then, Pargeter was no longer young. There was some talk in the neighborhood when I stayed on as housekeeper, you see. No reason there should have been. It was all aboveboard, but Pargeter was lonesome, and we spent a good bit of time together. Our neighbor, Lord Malton, tipped Harold the clue we were causing a scandal. Said he must either marry me or turn me off. So Harold offered, and I accepted. I'd be a fool not to, eh?"

"Surely Lord Pargeter is too old for that sort of scandal."

"He was seventy-two when I married him."

"And you only forty-one! Why did you not tell me you were getting married?"

"Being in mourning, we did it up quietly. And, my dear, to tell the truth, I was ashamed of myself, for there was a deal of talk in the neighborhood. I meant to write to you, but then Harold took ill, and I was fully occupied with that."

"I hope he is better?"

"Oh no, I buried him two months ago," she said blandly.

"Oh, I am sorry," Jane said uncertainly. Her uncertainty was caused by the lack of any show of sorrow in the widow.

Fay nodded. "It was not a love match, but I miss the old scoundrel. If I had ever dreamed I would have to face all this alone, I doubt I would have agreed to his terms."

"What terms were those, Auntie?"

"Fine lords and ladies always have strings attached to their contracts, including marriage. I agreed to remain in residence until—well, for a long time, so I am stuck with it. The fact is, the neighbors have sent me to Jericho. No one calls. I am alone, rattling around in this great house with only the servants to talk to. I want you to be my companion."

"It is fate," Jane said, and rose to throw her arms around her aunt. "I have my trunks with me."

"Excellent! But what were you up to, minx, that they turned you off?"

Jane explained the situation. "And is it really true I will never have to teach again? It's like a dream."

"It's pleasant here, but it's not all a bed of roses."

Jane looked around at the magnificent surroundings, at her aunt's lavish gown and jewelry, and said, "If this is not a bed of roses, I should like to know what is." With Lord Pargeter gone, there was nothing left to wish for in her new home.

"Roses have thorns, Jane. The particular thorn that bedevils me is Lady Sykes, and what business it is of hers, I should like to know. She is only a connection of Pargeter's. He didn't even bother to notify her of our marriage, but as soon as she learned of his death, she came pelting down, expecting to inherit Wildercliffe, for it was not entailed."

"She is some kin to the Pargeters, you say?"

"She is nobody; her papa was a yeoman farmer. She married Pargeter's cousin, Sir James Sykes.

Sir James is dead. It is her son that she hoped to see the heir. The more fool she! Pargeter loathed Nigel."

"Lady Sykes cannot upset the apple cart. You are genteel. I mean there was nothing irregular in the marriage, was there?"

Lady Pargeter's fingers plucked nervously at the velvet of her skirt. "Only the irregularity of Harold marrying his housekeeper. It is irregular, but not illegal. She hasn't a leg to stand on, and so I told her."

"She will soon tire of pestering you and go away."

"The woman sticks like a barnacle. She is turning the neighborhood against me. She has been billeting herself on Swann for a month, and has hired a lawyer to try to frighten me into submission."

"Swann? Is he some kin to Pargeter as well?"

"He was Lizzie's cousin—Lady Pargeter, you know. She was a Swann before marriage, but she was also kin to Pargeter. You know how these noble families are. Scawen Swann gave me no trouble at all. He is an easygoing sort of fool. Anyhow, I am all alone here, and want you to stay with me until—well, for as long as it suits you. Will you do it, Jane? You are the only relative I have in the world."

"With pleasure, but I can't help you with Lady Sykes. I know nothing of the law. Why do you not hire a lawyer?"

"Not necessary. Pargeter was as clever as can stare. She'll not break the will. I shall hire a lawyer if it comes to a court case. Thus far Lady Sykes is only threatening, and trying to work up a case against me. I would not give her the satisfaction to think I take her seriously. But enough of my troubles. Now let us discuss the happier side of my situation. I was left very well to grass, you must know."

"Yes," Jane said, gazing around in stupefaction.

"Fifty thousand, on top of the estate, and a handsome income as well from the tenant farms. All mine for life."

"A pity Lord Pargeter hadn't a son to carry on his name."

"Yes," Fay said, and immediately changed the subject. "Naturally I shall pay you."

"Miss Prism paid me fifty a year, plus room and board."

A merry peal of laughter rang out. "Skint! I was paid two hundred when I was Lizzie's companion, and I didn't have to lift a finger except to summon a servant. Fifty wouldn't keep you in ribbons here. We shall say two hundred for starters. How is that? I shall give you your first installment this very day."

"It's too much!"

Fay smiled. "Get used to it. I don't mean to keep myself locked away. Until my mourning is up, I cannot go flaunting myself in public, but I can entertain a few guests to dinner, and visit friends, now that I have a cohort. And you will be with me, rigged out like a fine lady. I'll not be cowed by Lady Nose-in-the-air Sykes. Dammed if I will. There! I should not have said that. It was Pargeter who got me in the habit. Now that I have a vicar's daughter to keep me in line, I shall soon be as nice as a nun again."

"A vicar's daughter and a schoolmistress."

"Pargeter said we were all fools, Jane, when I talked to him about our family. A clever man like your papa ought to have gone up to London and become a politician. You would not have been left penniless when he died. And you should have got yourself into a noble house where you would meet some interesting gentlemen."

"A gentleman is not likely to marry a governess, Auntie."

"I know one who married his housekeeper, and she was not young and pretty like you—although she was not too old to catch a gentleman's eye." On another peal of laughter, she called Broome to show Miss Lonsdale to the Rose Guest Suite.

"I shall let you get settled in. We dine at six. All we fine ladies dress for dinner. One never knows, Lady Sykes might set fire to the house. I would not give her the satisfaction of catching me without a string of diamonds around my neck."

Jane followed Broome upstairs to an elaborate suite of such splendor, she was half afraid to touch anything. It looked like a palace, after the humble room she had shared with a fellow teacher, Harriet Stowe, at Miss Prism's Academy.

She wandered about the bedroom and sitting room, marveling at the size and richness of the space. The sheen of rose brocade on the canopied bed and at the windows cast a glow on the carved mahogany furnishings. Her feet sank into the thick wool of an Oriental carpet. A servant had unpacked while she sat below with Fay. Her few gowns did not take up a quarter of the armoire, and her tortoiseshell comb and brush looked forlorn on the toilet table. How very different life was going to be, here at Wildercliffe.

And how very odd that Aunt Fay was mistress of it all. Jane could understand Fay's marrying

Pargeter for security, and for all the luxury his money brought. What she could not comprehend was why Pargeter had married Fay. Why not marry a younger lady, who might give him an heir? Or at least a lady from his own class of society. And he had not only married her, he had done it within a year of his wife's death. Of course, Pargeter was accustomed to having Fay about the place. To avoid scandal, he had married her—and within a few months Fay had ended up the inheritor of the whole fortune. Jane could easily understand that Lady Sykes was miffed. It did seem unfair.

Chapter Two

At Swann Hall, a very impatient Lady Sykes yanked at her shawl and scowled at her host as if it were his fault that she was so frustrated. Lady Sykes had been pretty once, but decades of greed and quarreling had left their mark on her face. Sharp lines were etched between her eyebrows and at the corners of her green eyes. Her auburn hair was streaked with silver, but it was her petulant lips, clamped in an angry, determined line, that lent her the air of a bulldog.

"Must you slouch in that ill-bred manner, Horace?" she said sharply to her brother.

Horace Gurney was possibly even more eager than the lady's host to see the back of her. The malleable Scawen Swann had allowed Horace, a mere connection, to billet himself at Swann Hall for the past decade. Despite the difference in their ages, the gentlemen rubbed along smoothly. If Scawen's wine cellar had to be restocked more often than formerly, he was too kind to say so.

"Any word from Belton on Fay Rampling?" Horace inquired. Belton was the lawyer she had hired to check up on Lady Pargeter, in hopes of discovering some irregularity in the infamous marriage.

Lady Sykes bridled up like an angry mare. "I

have it on the best authority she fed poor Harold wine from morning to night. No doubt she called in a preacher while he was in his cups and did the deed. It is nothing else but coercion, and as soon as Belton can get one of the footmen or maids to corroborate it, I shall have her taken before a magistrate."

Swann poked the dying embers and said in an amiable way, "Nothing in that, I fear. Harold was always a bit of a toper, beginning with ale for breakfast, through to a jug of brandy before hitting the tick at night. Mind you, he held his spirits like a gentleman."

"Nothing wrong with a wee drop," Horace said, tilting the wine decanter into his glass.

Lady Sykes directed one withering look of disgust at her brother. He looked little better than a groom, in his wrinkled jacket and with that unkempt head of gray hair. He was the image of their papa, a hulking man with no elegance and no manners. Lady Sykes preferred to forget her ancestors. Thank God Horace made his home with Scawen, or she would be lumbered with him in London.

"It was the brandy that rotted Pargeter's brain," she announced. "Pargeter must have been insane to marry her. Insanity is an excellent excuse to overturn the will. And who performed the ceremony? I made sure it was Vicar Hellman, but he tells me he knew nothing of the marriage until he heard it from Lord Malton. They did not post any banns. That looks fishy. I doubt they were ever legally married at all."

"Special license, I believe," Scawen said, with a kindly smile. "Perfectly legal."

Lady Sykes snorted. "I shall ask Belton to look into it." She rose, gathering her shawl around her, to retire.

Phoebe regularly retired to her chamber at nine on the dot to fire off a barrage of scolding letters to all her near and dear. The gentlemen agreed they could not cope with her were it not for those few free hours at the end of the day. They exchanged a sorry look when the door knocker sounded. Nine was late for a caller, but not too late for Belton, and his calls always put Phoebe in a pucker. Lady Sykes resumed her seat, mentally arraying accusations, complaints, questions, and demands to put to Belton.

Morton, the butler, appeared at the door of the saloon. "Lord Fenwick," he announced.

Lady Sykes leapt from the sofa as if she had been goaded by a cattle prod. "Lord Fenwick! What the devil is he doing here? Show him in, Morton." She turned to Swann, adding, "You ought to speak to that butler, Scawen. Leaving Lord Fenwick standing in that drafty hall, and in a soiled jacket, too."

"Fenwick never wore a soiled jacket in his life," Scawen chided her. "A regular out and outer."

"Morton never wore a clean one." She said no more, for she had to compose her face into a smile to greet Lord Fenwick, who was top of the trees.

To describe his appearance did not do him justice. He was of sufficient height and breadth of shoulders to qualify as well built. While not excessively handsome, his features were regular and pleasantly arranged: well-barbered brown hair, clever gray eyes, a straight nose, good teeth. His jackets, while impeccably cut, did not soar to any Olympian heights of dandyism. Yet with no outstanding features, he still managed to create a special air of consequence. His breeding showed in his easy manners, which never gave offense—unless he wished to.

Lady Sykes had never quite managed to trace his relation to herself, but as they were both connected to Pargeter, she claimed kinship, and made the most of it.

"Fenwick! What a delightful surprise!" she gushed. "Do come in. Should you not be in London, enjoying the Season?"

Fenwick advanced gracefully across the room and made his bows all around. Then he lifted Phoebe's hand and bestowed a kiss above it. "I followed my heart—to you, dear Cousin Phoebe. What should the ton be discussing but your absence?"

She lapped it up like a hungry cat taking cream. "Flatterer! Who would miss poor old me?"

"I not only missed you, my dear, but was so upset I asked Nigel where you were sequestering yourself, and came darting, *ventre à terre*, at once to find you."

"Chasing after a filly, in other words," Scawen said.

"*Au contraire*, Cousin."

"Eh? What do you mean?"

"He means a filly is chasing after him, ninnyhammer," Lady Sykes translated.

Fenwick smiled a bland smile. "Actually, I am on my way to my hunting box. It is no matter. I am here. Let the revels begin." He took a seat beside Phoebe. "What brings you to the wilds of Wildercliffe, Phoebe? Taking up hunting, are you?"

"Don't be ridiculous. How should I pay for a hunter?"

"With money, like the rest of us. You have plenty of it."

As Lady Sykes had been flaunting her imaginary poverty as a pretext for challenging Pargeter's will, she replied nobly, "I am poor as a church mouse, Fenwick."

"Ah, lost it all upon 'Change, did you? Pity," he said, with an air of utter indifference.

"Call for the good wine, Scawen," she said.

"You make me feel as if I were at a wedding at Cana," Fenwick murmured. "Actually, I would prefer tea, if it is not too much trouble."

"Coming right up," Scawen said, and pulled the bell cord.

Nothing was ever too much trouble for Scawen Swann. He was built low to the ground, like a badger. His sandy hair grew in a cowlick that no amount of brushing or water or oil could subdue. Jackets had a way of turning to wrinkles and spots as soon as they touched his back. He looked like a tramp, but his undemanding nature and generosity made him the most popular gentleman in the county.

"Can you stay a day or two?" Scawen asked.

It suited Lord Fenwick very well to remain incommunicado for a few days. A certain Lady Alice Merton was hot on his trail. He had claimed urgent business in Bath to escape her. His mama had retired there for the water. But as Lady Alice knew his mama, he had stopped at Bath only long enough to tell Lady Fenwick what he was up to.

"Go to your hunting lodge," his mama had suggested. "She will not be brass-faced enough to follow you there uninvited."

He felt Mama was a little optimistic in the matter. Lady Alice had followed him from London to Brighton, and had spoken of visiting cousins in Bath when he told her where he was going. She might very well show up at his lodge, but she could not ferret him out here as he had suppressed Swann's name.

"Of course, Fenwick will remain a few days," Lady Sykes informed her host. "Give him the Gold Suite next to mine, Scawen. The south end of the house is less drafty."

Fenwick gave a mischievous smile. "Take care, Phoebe, or our little secret will be out."

She responded with a coy smirk. If any of her friends had made such a suggestive comment, she would have given him a sharp rebuke. As Fenwick was a wealthy marquess, the remark was not only tolerated but would be repeated to her friends, and especially her many enemies, when she returned to civilization.

"Nigel tells me your visit has to do with old Pargeter's death," Fenwick said. "Made you his heir, has he? I made sure Soames would be his beneficiary."

It was like a spark to tinder. "What need has Harold Soames of money, I should like to know? He's rich as Croesus. Pargeter did not leave myself or Nigel a single sou!" she announced, eyes flashing. "Within months of poor Lizzie's death, he married his housekeeper under extremely odd circumstances and left her the lot—Wildercliffe, a fortune of at least fifty thousand, to say nothing of Lizzie's jewelry. I should say the housekeeper *claims* Harold married her. No one has seen the marriage certificate. The local vicar did not marry them, for I asked him."

Scawen said, "Special license, justice of the peace." No one paid him any attention.

A frown pleated Fenwick's brow. "This wants looking into," he said. "You ought to hire a lawyer."

"I have already hired a fellow called Belton."

"What does he say?"

"He is looking into it," she said unhappily. "The whole neighborhood is up in arms against the woman. Lord Malton does not visit her, and he, you must know, was Pargeter's bosom bow. She is invited nowhere. She must be talking to the walls, for she sees no one but the servants."

Scawen cleared his throat and said, "Did I mention she has a visitor? I saw Pargeter's traveling carriage coming from the direction of Bath this afternoon. A young lady got out at Wildercliffe. Had some trunks with her."

Lady Sykes turned pale. "You never told me so!"

"You never asked."

"You know I am keenly interested in everything that goes forth at Wildercliffe. What was she like, this so-called lady?"

"She was youngish," Scawen said.

There followed a ten-minute futile discussion about who the visitor could be. In the end, Lord Fenwick suggested they should call on the soi-disant Lady Pargeter the next morning to discover it for themselves.

"I shall send Belton. We do not call on the house-keeper," Lady Sykes said haughtily.

"The more fool you," Fenwick said. "Assuming the housekeeper did marry Pargeter, it is clear as glass that she coerced him in some manner. He was past seventy. I wonder if he was *compos mentis* at the time of the wedding."

"The very fact that he married his housekeeper is enough to tell you his brain was addled," she said angrily.

"Has Belton looked into this possibility?"

"The devil of it is that Pargeter seldom left home after Lizzie's death, so no one saw him. The servants are sticking by the housekeeper—one of their own, you see. They are all in it together, and living like kings on Pargeter's money."

"If Pargeter had reverted to childhood in his last year, there might be some indication of it about the place," Fenwick said. "Toys in his room, or scribbling on the walls . . ."

"She has got rid of any such evidence. Belton says they put on a good show when he calls. She suggested he go ahead and lay charges, and she would hire her own lawyer. Meanwhile, she would answer no more questions. The last time he called, she refused to see him. The impertinence of the creature!"

"It certainly wants looking into," Fenwick said. "I shall call on Lady Pargeter tomorrow. Will you come with me, Phoebe?"

"That I will not! I wouldn't give her the satisfaction, but you go by all means, dear Fenwick. You are sharp as a bodkin. You will see if anything is amiss. I am curious, as well, to hear a report on her new cohort. If you can discover her name, Belton will look into her background."

Fenwick was concerned at what he had heard. He was aware of Lady Sykes's habit of exaggerating matters and imagining wrongs, but it did seem suspicious that the exceedingly wealthy and top-lofty Lord Pargeter had married his housekeeper. If there had been any havey-cavey business about it, it should be cleared up. It would enliven his visit to look into the matter.

One did not retire at Swann Hall without inquiring of the host for his swans. Some men took pride in their families, or their cattle, some in their horses. For Scawen, swans were his reason for existence.

"How do the swans go on, Scawen?" he asked.

Scawen shook his head. "Terrible. We are down to two pairs—and of course, their cygnets. And of the two pairs, Darby and Joan are old as the hills. That leaves only Wilkie and Minerva. We lost our black swans, Diablo and Dorothy. Black swans were to be my contribution to Swann Hall. Papa built the conservatory; Grandpapa built the belvedere. I can't think of anything else to build." Swann Hall was a huge, rambling house built in a variety of styles, all managing to cohere into one interesting, if not beautiful, whole.

"What happened to the other swans?" Fenwick asked.

"I suspect the poachers took a couple of pairs. Henri and Rita died of old age. Bertie was used to sleep on the road—for the warmth in the paving stones, you know. A carriage got him one night. And some of 'em flew away. When Darby and Joan go, I am down to a pair. What is Swann Hall without swans?"

They discussed the securing of the remaining swans for half an hour. Scawen had run off the poachers, but why the swans were leaving was still to be determined.

"We shall have a look tomorrow," Fenwick said.

"I wish you would, Fen, for you know the old legend. When the swans die out, the Swanns die out as well."

"Don't be an idiot, Scawen," Lady Sykes snapped. "Of course, if the swans die, the swans die."

"No, but I mean the *Swanns*," Scawen said.

"With a capital *S*, Phoebe," Fenwick translated. "And a double *n* at the ending."

"Rubbish, you are thinking of the swans at Longleat," she declared.

"There have never been Swanns at Longleat," Scawen said, becoming annoyed.

"No swans at Longleat? Why, they're famous."

"Again, Swanns with a capital *S*," Lord Fenwick informed Phoebe.

"And furthermore," Scawen added, for he was becoming testy at Lady Sykes's overbearing manner, "if Pargeter left his blunt to anyone, it's more likely he would leave it to me than Nigel, for I was like a son to him. He didn't care for me in the least. Always told me I was a fool—just like Papa."

A raucous snort from the far sofa told them Gurney had fallen asleep. His sister looked at him with loathing. "Dear Horace—he has fallen asleep," she said, smiling at Fenwick. "I should retire as well. And you must be fagged after your trip, Fenwick. I shall speak to Morton about the Gold Suite."

She left, and the gentlemen settled in for some masculine conversation about horses and boxing matches and politics.

Chapter Three

At Wildercliffe, Jane awoke to see sunlight filtering through the rose window hangings. She leapt up with a gasp of alarm and reached for her watch. Eight-thirty! She would be late for class! Then she shook herself fully awake and lay back against the soft down pillow, smiling at her great fortune. She could sleep in this beautiful, soft, warm bed in this marvelous bedchamber until noon if she chose. Yet she was eager to be up and doing.

There was so much to explore and so much to discuss with her aunt that she rose at once. What luxury to pull a cord and have hot water delivered to your room. Meg, one of the young maids, brought her tea. "To get you going," she said. "And if you want a girl to help you dress, ma'am, you've only to say so."

Jane declined the offer and made her own modest toilette. At school she wore dark gowns, but the sunlight streaming through the window told her it was spring, and she reached for her blue mulled muslin. It was too wrinkled to wear, however, so she put it and a few other items aside for pressing and wore the dark blue serge gown she wore at school, adding her Sunday fichu of lace at the throat and her late mama's sardonyx cameo brooch.

As her aunt was still in bed, she ate alone in the breakfast room, which looked out on a formal rose garden. After a quarter of an hour, the silence began to close in on her. She could understand what Fay meant by the thorns in this rose bower she had inherited. It was the thorn of lonesomeness. Even the servants didn't speak. They crept up on silent feet, to appear suddenly at your elbow, holding a coffeepot or a rack of toast.

A much noisier breakfast was going forth at Swann Hall. After breakfast, it was only Lord Fenwick and Swann who headed out for Wildercliffe, Fenwick mounted on his chestnut hacker and Swann on a large, docile gray mare that just suited his temperament. Lady Sykes was eager to get into the house, but insisted she would not give the housekeeper the satisfaction of a call. What "satisfaction" a call from the termagant could bring required a deal of imagination. There was no question of Horace Gurney visiting Wildercliffe. He never went anywhere unless under duress, and seldom left his bedchamber before noon.

Swann Hall and Wildercliffe sat on opposite ends of a long, crescent-shaped lake. Fenwick had been to Wildercliffe a few times in the past, but as he visited dozens of stately homes, he had no sharp memory of it. Like Jane, he was surprised anew at its magnificence. His keen eyes observed that, whatever the character of the new Lady Pargeter, she had not let the estate deteriorate. The crops and flock were prospering; the fences were maintained, the tenant farms in good repair. Pargeter would have had a good bailiff, of course.

"Lady Pargeter ain't as bad as Phoebe says," Scawen mentioned, as they rode along.

"One always takes Phoebe's tendency to exaggerate into account," Fenwick said, "but it's deuced odd that Pargeter married an underbred woman, and so soon after his wife's death. And left one of the finest estates in the country to his housekeeper, who had been his wife for only a few months. You don't suspect foul play?"

"Eh?"

"Do you think it possible this Rampling woman was involved in Pargeter's death?"

"It never ever entered my head. Why would she do that?"

"To hasten along her inheritance. Why else would she marry a man in his seventies?"

"Maybe she liked him. Seems hard to believe, but there's no accounting for taste. Sykes married Phoebe. Lizzie liked Pargeter. Lizzie liked Miss Rampling, too. Bosom bows."

"Was Rampling at the house long?"

"A decade, give or take a year."

"Where did she come from?"

"She never said, but she seemed genteel whenever I had anything to do with her. Lizzie always said she didn't know how she could get along without Rampling. I daresay Pargeter felt the same."

Miss Rampling sounded like a cunning rogue to Fenwick. The manipulative sort of woman who knew how to make herself essential to an aging couple. A woman who came from nowhere and ended up queen of the castle in a decade had to be uncommonly sly, to say the least.

* * *

At Wildercliffe, Lady Pargeter had joined Jane in the morning parlor. It was she who spotted the callers from the breakfast room as they approached through the meadow.

"Scawen Swann is coming!" she exclaimed in some excitement. "He used to be a regular visitor when Lizzie and Pargeter were alive, but he has not come since Lady Sykes battened herself on him. I wonder what mischief he is up to. There's someone with him. Could it be—no, it's not Belton."

Jane hastened to the window to get a preview of the callers. Fay pointed out Swann, but it was at the other rider that Jane looked. He was every inch a gentleman and looked very dashing mounted on a prime piece of horseflesh, with his curled beaver tilted jauntily over one eye. The straight shoulders and head held high gave him an uncommonly proud air.

"Who is the other gentleman?" she asked, as the pair drew closer.

"Would it be Nigel Sykes, all grown up, I wonder? I've not seen him for five years. Let us greet them in the Blue Saloon, Jane. There's not time to clear away our breakfast here."

The ladies rushed into the grand chamber, to be found idly thumbing through magazines when Broome announced, "Lord Fenwick and Mr. Swann."

"Show them in, Broome," Lady Pargeter said in a haughty voice, with a wink at Jane. "It's not Nigel, thank God," she added aside.

Jane was nervous at the prospect of meeting a lord. She knew from her days at Miss Prism's that lords could cause no end of bother. When the gentlemen were shown in, her vague concern crystallized to alarm. She scarcely looked at Swann; one glance at his rather simple, smiling face told her he was harmless.

It was Lord Fenwick who caught her attention. First she observed that he was taller than average, and wearing an exquisitely tailored jacket of blue Bath cloth. She had never seen a cravat arranged so impeccably, nor top boots gleam so brightly. But she had been right that he was proud. Pride and suspicion marred what was otherwise a handsome face. She knew by his sharp expression and his darting, clever eyes that he was bent on mischief.

After a cursory examination of her aunt, those steel-hard eyes turned to examine her. She had been raked from head to toe by men before, most recently by Fortini. Lord Fenwick's examination was not of that sort. It was cold, insolent. She felt her spine stiffen, and her dutiful smile of welcome dwindle to annoyance.

Scawen Swann introduced his houseguest. Fenwick had been expecting the "housekeeper" would be a common sort of woman, overdressed and underbred. He was surprised to encounter a modest-looking lady. She was not dripping in diamonds, or sitting with her legs crossed, or drinking brandy. When his eyes turned to her cohort, he found an even more interesting female.

It was only the wary, angry expression on Miss Lonsdale's face that gave him any cause for suspicion, for her appearance was unexceptionable. Her blue eyes gazed at him from beneath long lashes. She wore her soft brown hair bundled neatly back from her face. Her complexion was of a ladylike pallor, and her demeanor was modest. Her dark blue gown was almost excessively so. She looked like a typical poor relation, or a governess. In fact, the whole scene was so genteel, it might have been set up to impress a caller. They would have seen him and Swann coming through the meadow.

Lady Pargeter presented her companion. "This is my niece, Miss Lonsdale. She has come to stay with me."

The group took up their positions around the grate.

Fenwick composed a cool smile and said, "Where do you come from, Miss Lonsdale?" He noticed the question displeased her. Why should she hesitate to reply, unless there was something discreditable in her background?

"From Bath," she said.

"Is your family still there?"

"My parents are dead," she said.

"Ah, then you lived with relatives?"

"I was employed in a lady's academy," she said. She was loath to mention the name Miss Prism, and added, "My aunt has invited me to stay with her."

"A schoolteacher, was you?" Scawen inquired.

"Yes," she said, with an angry look at Swann. Did he think she was the cook, or scrubbed floors?

"What academy was that, Miss Lonsdale?" Fenwick inquired.

She gave him another hostile look. The man was a bulldog. Any mention of her leaving the academy was painful; she did not want the local folks to discover her disgrace. Yet she had been trained as a young lady to be polite, and as a vicar's daughter to tell the truth. "Miss Prism's Academy for Young Ladies," she said.

"I have heard of it," Fenwick said, with a note of

surprise in his well-modulated voice. It was known to be very prestigious, and very strict. If Miss Lonsdale did indeed come from Miss Prism's, there could be nothing amiss in her background except poverty, and that, while unfortunate, was in no way immoral. In fact, it was almost a guarantee of integrity—*if* she had really taught there. . . .

"Were you there long?" he asked.

Something in his insolent, questioning look caused a stab of anger. She took a deep breath to control the sharp retort that longed to come out. "Eighteen months, two weeks, and three days," she said. "Are you interested in precise dates, milord?"

He ignored her gibe. "And before you joined Miss Prism?" he asked.

Lady Pargeter had had enough. "My niece is not applying for a position with you, milord," she said. "Is there some reason for this interrogation?"

Fenwick decided on the spot that he must watch his step with these "ladies." They knew what they were about. Any show of servility on their part would have suggested wrongdoing. He had merited that rebuke, and the "housekeeper" was not slow to deliver it. She wouldn't be browbeaten into compliance. The alternative was to dump the butter boat on her. A warm smile lit his eyes and lifted the corners of his lips.

"Forgive me," he said, directing his words to both ladies. "Curiosity has always been my besetting sin. I came to pay my respects to Lord Pargeter's widow." He turned to direct his next words to Jane. "I am a cousin to Pargeter. I was trying to determine whether we might have met before, ma'am. I am sorry if my questions struck you as an interrogation. My mama makes her home in Bath. I often visit her." His interest soared when Jane gave a wince at that piece of information.

The charm of his smile was ignored in this dreadful piece of information. "I have heard of Lady Fenwick. I've never met her," Jane said. But Lady Fenwick might very well have heard of her by now. Many of the students were from noble families. The dismissal of a schoolmistress on moral grounds would provide a small item of gossip. "Do you have relatives—cousins or nieces—at Miss Prism's, milord?" she asked warily.

"Not at the moment," he said, and watched as the tension eased out of her face. His suspicions heightened when she smiled in relief.

"I thought they might have attended Miss Prism's," she said.

"Not within the past eighteen months, two weeks, and three days," he replied, with a glinting, sly smile that set her nerves on edge. Almost a challenging smile. What had he heard?

Lady Pargeter decided it was time to change the subject. "You are staying with Swann, Lord Fenwick?"

"Just so. I am visiting for a few days and couldn't leave without calling on you. How do you go on, Lady Pargeter?"

"As well as I can, being cut off from the world," she said, with a sharp glance at Swann, who was harboring the lady responsible for her isolation, and well he knew it.

Scawen paid her no heed. He had discovered that Miss Lonsdale was a nice, quiet sort of lady. Pretty without flaunting herself. He wanted a wife, and felt that his best chance of procuring one was to find some undiscovered violet growing unseen, and rush her off to Vicar Hellman before she caught someone else's eye.

"Would you like to see my swans, Miss Lonsdale?" he asked.

"Where are they?" she asked in some little confusion.

"At Swann Hall. That is to say, on the lake. Only a few of them left."

"Yes, I should like to see them sometime," she said vaguely.

"Tomorrow. I shall call on you tomorrow. Don't wear a good dress. What you have on will be fine. And you'll need some stout shoes, for it's wet in the water. In the rushes, that is to say."

Jane blinked, wondering how to respond to this news that water was wet, and to the slight on her good serge gown.

Seeing her plight, Fenwick came to the rescue, hoping to lure her into friendship, and eventually into revelations. "It will be chilly by the lake. You will want that nice warm gown," he said.

"Oh yes." She smiled, surprised that he should come to her rescue, and grateful for his finesse.

The conversation came to a temporary halt. She noticed Fenwick direct a commanding look on Mr. Swann, and sat on nettles, waiting to see what occurred next.

Chapter Four

There had been some discussion between the gentlemen as to how they might discover clues to Pargeter's mental condition just prior to his death. They agreed that the master bedroom was the likeliest place to find them. Fenwick had convinced Swann that he was the more likely one to request a visit thither.

When Fenwick gave him a commanding look, Swann said, "We was wondering if we might have a peek at the master bedroom." Lady Pargeter stared at him in astonishment. "Only if you ain't using it yourself, of course," he added.

"It happens I am not. It's too dark to suit me, but may I know why you wish to view it?"

Swann had been coached. "Old times' sake," he replied. "Many's the time I have enjoyed a gargle of brandy there with old Pargeter when he was racked up with gout, you know. I would like to see his last resting place—while he was alive, I mean, for of course, I often visit his grave. Well, two or three times. Once, actually, but I took some flowers."

Fenwick saw he had overestimated Swann's potential as a conspirator. "Actually, Swann was hoping for a keepsake, Lady Pargeter. Nothing valuable like his watch, but some trifle—a favorite book of poetry, perhaps, in which he had jotted down his thoughts."

"Pargeter never read a poem in his life," Lady Pargeter said comprehensively. "He was reading the *Farmer's Almanac* the day before he died. I gave it to the bailiff. There was an article on some new sheep Pargeter meant to discuss with him. If you would like a cravat pin, I would be happy to give you one as a memento. I shall ask Broome to fetch it."

"Allow me," Swann said, with a triumphant smile at Fenwick. "I know just where he kept them."

Fenwick noticed that Lady Pargeter and Jane exchanged a meaningful look.

They both realized there was some mischief afoot. Fay knew that Swann hadn't a sentimental bone in his body. He was no blood relation to Pargeter, nor had they been especially close. Swann's mama and Lady Pargeter had been cousins—but he hadn't wanted any keepsake of Lizzie. What he wanted was to get into Pargeter's bedroom and snoop to see what he could find to take back to Lady Sykes and her lawyer. Not that he would find anything.

"Miss Lonsdale will go with you," Fay said, with a gracious nod of her head.

"Very kind of you," Swann replied, smiling fondly at Jane. Fate seemed to be throwing the young lady into his path.

Fenwick rose when Jane stood up. As if on impulse, he said to Lady Pargeter, "May I accompany them above stairs?" When she frowned, he rushed in with an excuse. "I have not been at Wildercliffe for some years. I should like to refresh my memories of it. A fine house, Lady Pargeter."

"Certainly, Lord Fenwick. We shall all go," she said, and accepted his assistance from her seat.

She noticed the tightening of his jaw, which sat ill with his efforts at a smile. Oh yes, he was up to something, right enough, but he would have to get up early in the morning to outwit her.

The group, led by Lady Pargeter, proceeded up the grand staircase and along a corridor to the master bedroom. Swann walked with Jane behind Fay. Fenwick brought up the rear. He noticed how small Jane's waist was, and the interesting swaying of her hips. Over her shoulder, he made a few comments on paintings and carving as they went, to lend credence to his request to view the house.

Lady Pargeter entered the master bedroom first and drew back the heavy curtains. A rich but gloomy chamber came into view.

"I can see why you wouldn't want to sleep here after Pargeter died," Swann said. That struck him as implying the lady had enjoyed sleeping there with Pargeter. He felt he should modify it in some manner and added, "Not to say you enjoyed it *before* he died." This was even worse. "Not to say you *didn't* enjoy it. Not that it's any of my business one way or t'other," he finished, blushing.

"What beautiful carving!" Fenwick said, rather hastily, and walked forward to the canopied bed. "Grinling Gibbons, is it?" He ran his fingers over an indifferent carving of a vine crawling up the bedpost, to terminate in a griffin.

"I've no idea," Lady Pargeter said, rather snappishly, and strode to the dresser. "Here is Pargeter's trinket box. Help yourself, Mr. Swann."

Fenwick's sharp eyes darted around the room. He saw no evidence of senility. Everything was as it should be. But then, the chamber had obviously been tidied up after Pargeter's death. While Swann made his selection from the jewelry box, Fenwick lifted the skirt of the canopied bed and peered under it, thinking a toy might have escaped detection by the servants, but there was nothing there save the carpet. When he looked up, he saw Miss Lonsdale was observing him in a questioning way.

"I thought I saw a mouse," he said blandly.

If this was an excuse to get the ladies out of the room, it failed. "Indeed? And I thought I smelled a rat," she replied demurely.

A reluctant smile tugged at his lips. "At least you didn't say you saw one," he said.

She turned toward Swann and her aunt, for she was uncertain how to reply to this mischievous speech.

"Feel like a dashed beggar," Swann said, looking at the cravat pins, and trying to decide which was the least valuable. There were a few diamond ones and one ruby. He chose a small black pearl. "Very kind of you, Lady Pargeter. I will treasure this as a keepsake of old—of Pargeter."

"Would you also like a keepsake, Lord Fenwick?" Lady Pargeter asked.

"I find memories are the best keepsake," he said, and they returned below stairs.

Fenwick fell into step with Jane. "Will you be making your home permanently with your aunt," he asked, "or is this merely a sojourn between teaching positions?"

"I have no plans to return to teaching."

"That sounds very definite. Did you not enjoy it?"

"Would you?" she asked, and hastened on a step ahead of him before he could reply, for she disliked this line of questioning.

Lady Pargeter was uncertain how to treat Fenwick. If Lady Sykes had brought him in to cause mischief, she ought to give him short shrift. On the other hand, if he was just a casual visitor at Swann Hall, he might be of some use to her. Already he had brought Swann for a visit, and that must have taken some doing. If he could bring Lord Malton around, she would soon be established as respectable. She had no intention of apologizing for her marriage, but wondered if she might explain it in some manner that would make it more acceptable to him.

"Would you care for a cup of tea?" she asked.

Both gentlemen accepted with alacrity, and the tea was brought. Scawen began telling Jane about his swans. Before long, he had lured her to the window that gave a view of the lake. While he occupied Jane with a mild flirtation, Fay spoke to Fenwick, in her usual frank manner.

"Well, you have had a look at me now, milord," she said. "Am I as bad as Lady Sykes painted me?"

A spontaneous smile lit his eyes. "That would be difficult indeed, ma'am."

A bark of laughter greeted his words. "I know my marriage must have been a disappointment to her, but the fact is, Pargeter had no intention of leaving anything to Nigel. Nor is he such a fool as to have left the estate out of his own family forever. It is only mine during my lifetime."

"And after?" Fenwick asked, with equal frankness.

"It was Pargeter's wish that the terms of his will

remain secret for a year, but if it sets your mind at rest, I shall tell you this much. It reverts back to a relative of Pargeter's."

"Indeed!"

"I should not like you to get your hopes up, however. He didn't leave it to you."

"I didn't expect it," Fenwick said. His eyes turned to Swann. "As we are being quite open, do you mind my asking why you married him?"

"What you really want to know is why he married me. He was old and lonesome, and Lord Malton gave him the notion we were causing a scandal by living here together after Lizzie—Lady Pargeter—died. He was used to having me about. I had been Lizzie's companion for a decade. I went about everywhere with them, almost as one of the family. He didn't want me to leave, so he made an honest woman of me. If he had lived, it would have been a nine days' wonder. It was his death so quickly after we married that caused the mischief."

"What was the cause of his death?"

Lady Pargeter gave him a knowing look. "I did not feed him poison, if that is what she has hinted. It was his heart. He went off in the middle of the night. A quick, quiet death. The doctor signed the death certificate with no trouble. Would you like to see it?"

Fenwick listened, and found himself believing the story. "Of course not," he said, embarrassed.

Lady Pargeter was pretty, in a fulsome sort of way. She was genteel, if outspoken; Pargeter was accustomed to her. She would have provided familiar company to an elderly gentleman who was set in his ways. Pargeter's life and his fortune were his own, to do with as he wished. He would care nothing if his marriage caused a scandal in the neighborhood. It was only his untimely death that created the mischief. In short, Fenwick felt a perfect fool, and like a proper gentleman, he apologized.

"I am glad you came," Lady Pargeter said. "Naturally I would like to see my position in the neighborhood established on a normal footing. If Lady Sykes would care to call, she would be welcome."

"I shall give her the message. May I call again as well, Lady Pargeter?"

"I would be happy to receive you again."

He turned his attention to the window, where Scawen was pointing toward the lake, no doubt bethumping Miss Lonsdale with some swan lore.

"Minerva was so jealous she pecked at Dorothy till she had driven the poor pen away. As bad as Phoebe," Swann said.

Miss Lonsdale assumed Phoebe was another swan, and commiserated with him. "They sound very ill natured, to be sure, and they look so gentle and lovely," she said.

"Aye, they are trouble from beak to tail. They remind me of you, Miss Lonsdale." Jane looked at him in astonishment. Fenwick's lips quirked in amusement. "Really they are dashed pretty with those great long necks, like yours. They float along so gracefully, until they hit dry land, where they put a duck to shame for waddling."

"Thank you," Jane said, choking back a laugh. She had been speaking to Swann long enough to know there was no vice in him. He was trying to be complimentary.

Fenwick rose to take his leave. Glancing toward the grate, Jane saw he was gazing at her with suppressed laughter lighting his eyes. When their eyes met, he smiled in a conspiratorial way, as if sympathizing with her. The last trace of the proud lord had vanished from him. She felt an answering smile move her lips. A small warmth grew in her. Her past life had given few opportunities to meet gentlemen. She had never met anyone remotely like Lord Fenwick.

"It is time we should be leaving, Scawen," Fenwick said.

"I shall call for you tomorrow at ten, Miss Lonsdale," Swann said. "I look forward to it."

"Delightful, Miss Lonsdale," Fenwick said, shaking her hand and gazing directly into her eyes.

Jane was expecting a bow. Caught off guard, she didn't return the pressure, or the compliment, but just looked at him as if he were a riddle. She noticed how long his eyelashes were. His eyes were not really such a steely gray at close range. More like opals, with glinting flashes of light lurking in their depths.

"And Lady Pargeter," he added, turning to her aunt.

The gentlemen left, and the ladies poured themselves another cup of tea to discuss the visit.

Chapter Five

"What do you make of that?" Lady Pargeter asked. It was a rhetorical question. She proceeded at once to tell Jane what the visit was all about. "A fishing expedition. They came to see what they could discover. They hoped to get a look at the will in Pargeter's desk. What other reason could they have for wanting to go upstairs?"

"Fenwick was looking all around in an odiously curious way. He even peered under the bed."

"Did he indeed? He'd find nothing but dust."

"He might discover worse if he asks questions about me in Bath."

"That is the least of my concerns."

Jane looked alarmed. "Is there something you haven't told me about your marriage, Auntie?"

"No, no. The marriage is fine."

"Is there some secret about the will?"

"A part of it is not to be made public for a year. I told Fenwick about it."

She then proceeded to tell Jane the same thing, not revealing the identity of the mysterious inheritor, and moving rather vaguely over the phrase "providing certain conditions are met."

"What conditions?" Jane asked.

"Wills are written in legal mumbo jumbo with a

hundred heretofores and whereases. One hardly knows what it all means. You know what lawyers are."

The talk left her hungry, and she called for some bread and butter to tide her over until luncheon. While she devoured two slices of bread, she continued gossiping.

"Fenwick could be of some use to us, if we could ingratiate him. I believe I shall invite him to dinner."

Jane was happy to hear it. She didn't trust Fenwick an inch, but she was exhilarated at the prospect of seeing him again. He had come down off his high horse, just before he left. She wondered how he would behave on their next meeting.

"You can hardly invite Fenwick and not the others," she said. "It would look so very odd."

"I shall invite them all, including Lady Sykes— and pray that she doesn't come, but goes back to London, the pest."

The only other thing of interest that occurred at Wildercliffe that day was the discovery of a black pearl cravat pin on the table near where Swann had been sitting. This confirmed that he had no interest whatsoever in a memento from Pargeter. In the afternoon Fay had a nap and Jane went for a long walk about the estate. It offered enough interest that she scarcely gave a thought to Miss Prism's Academy, except to pity her friend Harriet Stowe and the other schoolmistresses who were still there, slaving their lives away.

It seemed lonesomeness was not going to be as much of a problem as she had feared. Already they had had two gentlemen calling. She was going out with Mr. Swann on the morrow, and now there was talk of a dinner party. She turned her mind to the vexing problem of what she could wear to impress the toplofty Lord Fenwick.

At Swann Hall, Lady Sykes was waiting on nettles to hear an account of the visit. "Well, what did you learn?" she demanded of Fenwick.

"We were looking for mares' nests," he scoffed. "There is nothing amiss with Lady Pargeter. I stopped to visit Lord Malton on the way home. He verified what Lady Pargeter told me. In fact, he was one of the witnesses at the wedding."

Fenwick explained how the wedding had come about. When this did not appease Lady Sykes, he mentioned the peculiar terms of the will.

"Rubbish!" the dame declared. "Whoever heard of a will not being read in full for a year? It is easy for her to say the estate will revert to Nigel."

"That is not what she said. It will not revert to Nigel, but to someone in Pargeter's family."

"Who else could it be? Much good it will do poor Nigel. The housekeeper is in her early forties. She might last half a century, racking up the income all the while. She will have a veritable fortune to leave to her niece. If Nigel dies young like his papa, he will never see a sou of his money."

"I would not encourage Nigel to believe the estate will ever be his," Fenwick said, and was completely ignored.

"It is a hum to calm our ruffled feathers," Phoebe declared. "She is breaking the news by degrees. In a year we will learn the whole has been left to the housekeeper with no strings attached."

"There is nothing you can do about it," Fenwick said. "She was legally married to Pargeter. The estate was not entailed. He was not mad, for Malton visited him the day he died, and Pargeter had a business discussion with his bailiff later that same day. The will is legal. Accept it, Phoebe, and make the best of it. You are only throwing good money after bad by proceeding with Belton."

Lady Sykes had a keen aversion to wasting any kind of money, good or bad. She was eventually talked into believing she might not succeed in unseating the housekeeper, and began to consider ways and means of making the best of it. Some sort of alliance by marriage with the housekeeper was one possibility, before Lord Malton beat them to it. It would give Phoebe access to Wildercliffe for visits and whatever she could pick up, and put the income in the hands of the husband. The husband must, therefore, be someone she could bear-lead. She looked at Horace, who sat nursing a glass of wine. No decent lady would so much as look at him, but the housekeeper seemed fond of marriage, and would not be fussy.

She turned to her brother. "You must make a bid for the housekeeper, Horace," she announced.

"A pretty woman, Fay Rampling," Horace said, with a wobbly smile. "I always had a fancy for her, to tell the truth. And old Pargeter had a wonderful cellar."

"There you are, then. Run a comb through your hair, put on a clean shirt, and go calling on her. She will have you, see if she don't. She is so fond of marriage."

"P'raps I will," Horace said, and picked up his glass.

"What was the niece like?" was Lady Sykes's next question. "I never heard of a Miss Lonsdale."

Swann considered Miss Lonsdale his department and replied, "Pretty. Funny."

Lady Sykes leapt on this crumb. "Pretty strange, was she?"

"Eh? No, damme. Pretty and strange—I mean funny—amusing."

"How old?"

"Youngish."

"About twenty-one," Fenwick added.

"She will freeze Horace out and have the lot to herself," Phoebe declared.

"Damme, Lady Pargeter can't marry her niece," Swann said angrily.

"Idiot! She can keep Rampling from marrying Horace. Is she well spoken?"

"Of course she is. She was a schoolmistress. Very genteel."

"Penniless, in other words. There is nothing so genteel as genteel poverty. A bundle of smirks and smiles, I wager."

"Not in the least. She's a lively gel, a real spark."

Lady Sykes frowned, deep in scheming, and turned her attention to a more credible witness. "What was your opinion, Fenwick?" She immediately noticed his hesitation in answering. "Something off there, was there?"

"She seemed reluctant to discuss her origins, and her recent past," he admitted, and told Phoebe what Jane had told him.

"Miss Prism's is unexceptionable," Phoebe declared. "Perhaps I should send for Nigel to divert Miss Lonsdale."

Fenwick swallowed a grin. "He will require a clever wife," he said mischievously.

"Nonsense, what he requires is a rich wife. I didn't mean that he should offer for the schoolteacher, but only divert her attention while Horace marries the housekeeper. Mind you, I don't trust this waiting a year to finish reading the will. It may very well be that the estate is entailed upon the schoolteacher."

"You missed your calling, Phoebe," Fenwick said with a satirical smile. "You should have been a general. Wellington could use you in the Peninsula."

Phoebe sat like a statue, staring with narrowed eyes at her fingers, which were curled into fists. "That's it!" she exclaimed, jumping up. "Miss Lonsdale is to be the heir. What a fool I was not to see it sooner."

"Lady Pargeter said the estate was to revert to the Pargeter family," Renshaw reminded her. "Malton confirmed it, though he was reluctant to do so."

"Of course he confirmed it. Are you all blind?" Phoebe asked, looking around the room. "Miss Lonsdale is Pargeter's daughter. It's plain as the nose on your face. She is his bastard daughter. You're too young to recall, Fenwick, but Pargeter was running around with a Miss Emily somebody from Bath twenty-odd years ago. Now, what was her last name? I don't think it was Lonsdale, but that is no matter. Bath, you see, where the schoolteacher comes from. He used to visit Bath regularly for two years. Lizzie knew full well he had a *chère amie*, but she didn't make a fuss. She never cared overly much for that sort of thing. She was a real lady.

"Pargeter has kept the girl under wraps all the while, hoping to have a son, but as he did not, he has decided to leave the lot to his bastard daughter. He married Rampling, pretending the girl is her niece, to have an excuse to bring her to Wildercliffe, and to cover her illegitimacy. That is why the chit is reluctant to discuss her origins."

Swann said, "Eh?" and demanded a few repetitions of the story. As it had already occurred to Fenwick, he had only a few objections.

"Miss Lonsdale doesn't look like the Pargeters," he said.

"She must take after her mama. You may be sure Miss Emily—what *was* her name?—she must have had something in the way of looks to attract Pargeter."

"Why would Pargeter have made his daughter work for her living? Miss Lonsdale was a schoolmistress," Fenwick said.

"If she was a schoolmistress, then she was educated, raised as a lady, in other words. Pargeter was playing it cagy, waiting to see if he had a son. He wanted the schoolteacher to be able to step into a lady's role if things fell out as they did, but to be prepared to look after herself if necessary."

"Skint!" Swann said angrily. "With all his blunt, he ought to have done more for Miss Lonsdale."

Lady Sykes rose from her favorite seat by the grate. "I shall send for Nigel at once. The schoolteacher is worth a mint. Fifty thousand, plus Wildercliffe and all its income! To say nothing of the jewelry."

"But Lady Pargeter has the estate and income until she dies," Horace asked.

"Yes, she has," Fenwick said firmly.

Phoebe stopped at the door and turned around. "I don't think Nigel would like that."

"You are leaping to conclusions, as usual, Phoebe," Fenwick said. "I believe Miss Lonsdale is Lady Pargeter's niece, as they claim. They have some similar look around the eyes."

"Then the schoolteacher must be a nasty-looking piece, but she might still be Pargeter's daughter. He was no Adonis, if you recall."

"Actually, Miss Lonsdale is quite pretty," Fenwick said musingly.

"Whatever she looks like, there must be some good reason Rampling hired her," Phoebe said, and went to her room to brood over the matter, and how she should proceed.

She must by all means avoid Nigel offering for the schoolteacher if she was *not* to inherit Wildercliffe. Overall, the safest course was to have Horace marry the housekeeper, for Rampling had undisputed claim to the estate and its income until she died. If, when the year was up, the will stated that Wildercliffe was entailed on Miss Lonsdale, then Nigel could marry her. In the meanwhile, she was not likely to meet any interesting gentlemen living here in the country. And she could hardly parade herself about London when the family was in mourning.

Phoebe was aware that her path was by no means clear. There was Malton, a widower, who knew exactly how the land lay, and might marry Rampling. He already had an estate and more blunt than he knew what to do with, however. He did not call on the housekeeper, so that was under control for the present.

Her pride did battle with her greed, and before

she left her room, she had decided to make the supreme sacrifice. She would give the housekeeper the satisfaction of a call on the morrow.

Chapter Six

The morning brought heavy skies and rain; not a brisk shower that might work itself out in a hurry, but a slow, desultory drizzle of the sort that continues for hours. Jane was not surprised to receive a note from Swann requesting a postponement of their outing to see the swans. What did surprise both Jane and her aunt was a tap at the door at about eleven, as the ladies sat in the Blue Saloon reading the journals. Lady Pargeter called Broome.

"If that is Belton, I'm not at home," she said.

It was not Lady Sykes's lawyer who soon entered the room, but Lady Sykes herself, draped in crape, and buttressed on one side by her brother, Horace, on the other by Swann, with Fenwick bringing up the rear. Lady Sykes had decided to be gracious, but to see that housekeeper reclining on a chaise longue in Nigel's house, wearing Lizzie's pearls and an enviably rich gown of black lutestring, was too much for her. It was all she could do to restrain herself from darting forward and snatching the pearls from the creature's throat.

"Lady Pargeter," she said in icy accents, and walked into the room, while her sharp eyes took an inventory of its fabulous appointments. Those Van Dycks alone were worth a fortune!

Lady Pargeter did not stir from her chaise longue, but only held out her hand as if, Phoebe said later, she were the pope granting an audience.

Phoebe ignored the hand. "You don't mind if we have a seat, milady?" she said, and sat on the chair farthest from her foe, while still within shouting distance of her.

"Help yourself, Lady Sykes," Lady Pargeter replied icily. "At your age, you would not want to be left standing for long. You're looking a little peaky."

That soon in the visit swords were crossed, but each lady had her own agenda, and tried to keep the damage to a minimum.

"Very true," Lady Sykes riposted, "at *our* age, we like to sit down." Lady Pargeter was the better part of a decade younger than her caller.

"Could I give you a glass of wine, Lady Sykes?"

"Wine, at this hour of the morning! Oh, I am not such a toper as that, milady," she replied, her eyes glancing off the decanter by Lady Pargeter's elbow. "But if you ask Broome for a cup of tea, I would be happy to accept it. Broome knows how I like it," she added, to bolster her claim to the place.

"Yes, he has an excellent memory," Lady Pargeter said. "When were you last here, Lady Sykes? Around the turn of the century, it must have been, for you have not called since I have been living here."

"It is possible I called and was not presented to the *servants*," Lady Sykes retorted.

"Nor to Lizzie, I assume, for I was her constant companion for a decade."

"How nice for you. And from there you became housekeeper—before becoming Lady Pargeter, I mean."

"My position was more that of *chatelaine*."

"Trust the French to have a word for it!"

Jane was on nettles, fearing the guest and hostess would soon come to blows. It was especially troublesome as these callers were their closest neighbors. She wished she could do something to cool the heated conversation. She cast a hopeful glance at Swann. He was brushing dust off his trousers and didn't see her. Her eyes turned to Fenwick. He appeared to be enjoying the exchange of insults, to judge by the unsteadiness of his lips. When she caught his eye, he winked.

He did come to the rescue, but in a manner that Jane feared would pitch her from the frying pan into the fire.

"You have not met Miss Lonsdale, Phoebe," he said, during a break in the insults. Jane cast one angry glare on him before rising.

She curtsied to Lady Sykes and said, "I am happy to meet you, ma'am."

She was amazed to receive a gloating smile in return. Lady Sykes indicated the chair beside her and said, "Do sit over here where we can become acquainted, my dear. I have been hearing so much about you."

"Really?" Jane asked in surprise. She darted a questioning look at Fenwick, then sat beside Lady Sykes.

"So you are a schoolmistress," Phoebe said, examining the girl for any resemblance to Pargeter. She soon thought she discerned a certain something in the conformation of the face bones. Whether she was Pargeter's bastard or not, it was clear Miss Emily—what *was* the woman's name?—

had convinced Pargeter she was, and the chit would end up mistress of Wildercliffe.

"Yes, ma'am, I was teaching in Bath until a few days ago, when Aunt Fay invited me to stay with her."

"At Miss Prism's, I understand." Jane nodded. "A very select school. You must have had someone very important to vouch for you, to secure a post there."

"The dean of Bath Abbey gave me a character. He knew my papa."

"Ah!"

"Papa was a vicar at Radstock, near Bath," Jane added, as her questioner seemed so curious.

"And is your papa still alive?"

"No, he was ill—dying really—when he spoke to the dean about finding me a position."

"You must have received a formidable education to be hired by Miss Prism. She demands French and Italian, I believe."

"She teaches French and Italian, but I taught only English. I don't speak Italian, and my French, I fear, is not good enough to teach."

"Such modesty!" Phoebe said, smiling in approval. "Was your mama also from Radstock?"

"Mama was from Bath."

Lady Sykes said, "Ah!" but she said it in a way that suggested *Aha!* A smile of satisfaction twitched at her pursed lips. "Was her Christian name, by any chance, Emily? The reason I ask—"

"No, ma'am. It was Patricia. Patricia Rampling. I am Fay—Lady Pargeter's—niece on my mama's side, you see."

Jane found it odd that her origins should be of such interest to Lady Sykes, but as it kept her from pestering Fay, she was content to answer questions. She noticed that Fenwick was listening quite as eagerly as her questioner. She had nothing to hide, as the inquisition didn't touch on her reason for leaving Miss Prism's Academy. Nor did Lady Sykes have much more to ask. She now had names, dates, and locations. Belton would look into it, and see if Miss Jane Lonsdale was not adopted. Phoebe's success put her in good humor. When the tea tray arrived, she released Jane.

"Come here and sit beside me, Swann," she ordered. "Let Horace entertain Lady Pargeter."

Horace was not loath to slide onto the chair so close to the wine decanter.

"None of that milksop for me," he said, declining tea and reaching for the wine. "We have missed you, Miss— Dear me, I keep forgetting you are a fine lady now. How do you like it?"

"I like it fine, Mr. Gurney," Lady Pargeter replied. As he was being friendly, she said, "What possessed your sister to call, after all this time?"

"We felt it was time to make it up."

"She seems mighty interested in my niece."

"Has her eye on Miss Lonsdale for Nigel, I believe."

This was the best joke Lady Pargeter had heard in some time. Phoebe would no more let Nigel marry a penniless vicar's daughter than she'd let him join the army. "And you have your eye on me, no doubt," she said, with a burst of laughter. She was amazed to see a guilty flush suffuse his wan cheeks.

He gave her a roguish look. "I won't say it hasn't occurred to me," he riposted.

So that's what the vixen is up to! Fay said to herself. *She thinks to plant old Gurney on me. The woman is mad as a hatter.* She went along with the flirtation, however, to amuse herself.

Fenwick noticed that Miss Lonsdale was at loose ends, and moved to join her, where she sat primly sipping her tea. Jane had been acutely conscious of his presence ever since the company's arrival. Despite his less than exemplary behavior the day before, she had been hoping for a few moments alone with him. Her heart thumped nervously as he took the chair beside her and gave her a quizzing smile.

"As we have been exchanging secret glances for quite ten minutes, the next step is for us to exchange a few words," he said.

She flushed when she realized that she had indeed been exchanging secret glances with this dashing lord. In her discomfort she spoke more bluntly than she liked. "Why did you draw Lady Sykes's attention to me?" she asked.

"Why did you look at me in that pleading way? I thought you were uncomfortable with the conversation, if one can call two cats hissing conversation. I was merely trying to divert the talk to less violent channels."

"I was uncomfortable, but I didn't mean for you to draw Lady Sykes's attention to me."

"I'm sure you were already the cynosure of all eyes, ma'am. It is the inevitable fate of the youngest, prettiest lady in the room." Jane gave a little snort of derision.

"Considering the competition, there is not much compliment in that comparison," he added. "I shall improve on my compliments as we go on. How was

I to know Phoebe would subject you to such a barrage of questions? It seems you attract interrogators, Miss Lonsdale," he said, smiling ruefully.

She replied, "I cannot imagine why I have suddenly incited so much curiosity, unless it is my relationship to Aunt Fay."

"I fancy you've hit the nail on the head."

"It's a pity the ladies cannot rub along better. Aunt Fay is lonesome here."

"She has you now. Such charming company must go a long way toward alleviating the situation." He sketched a small bow to accompany his compliment. Then he peered at her archly. "Was that better?"

Jane assumed this sort of flirtation was the accepted mode amongst fine lords and ladies, and smiled her approval. "Aunt Fay has no one of her own age. I think she misses Lizzie—Lady Pargeter, I should say."

"And not her late husband, Lord Pargeter?"

Jane found herself being examined by a pair of brightly curious eyes. "And Pargeter, of course, but a lady likes to have a female of her own age to discuss those things that are of interest only to ladies."

"I should think you're missing your friends as well, Miss Lonsdale. I am obviously not a female, and a decade older than you, but if you would like to discuss those things you imagine only ladies are interested in, I should be happy to try to oblige you."

"Oh, I am not lonesome yet."

"I am," he said bluntly. "Let us comfort and console each other with a good scandal broth. Now, where shall we begin our gossip? What do you think of Phoebe's bonnet? Did you ever see such a quiz?"

Jane's eyes widened in astonishment to hear such nonsense from Lord Fenwick. Her notion of him had been formed on his first visit when he had questioned her so brusquely, almost rudely. He hardly seemed to be the same man today.

Undeterred by her lack of response, Fenwick chatted on. "It would do well enough for a widow, but for a distant cousin to be donning such a load of crape is doing it too brown—or in this case, too black. Much good it will do her, unless Pargeter is looking down on her from above. And even then, he can hardly change his will."

He was rewarded by a small gurgle of laughter. "What is of more interest to me is Mr. Gurney's setting up a flirtation with my aunt," she said.

"Your wits are gone begging, ma'am. He's planning to root you out, limb and branch, and replace you as Lady Pargeter's companion. A curious notion of horticulture to be sure, to replace a healthy young rose with a withered stump of yew, but you will find no excess of intelligence at Swann Hall." He noticed that, instead of being flattered at being called a rose, she was regarding him with narrowed eyes. "Why are you looking at me like that?" he asked bluntly.

"I hadn't realized I was looking at you in an objectionable way, but as you ask, I wondered why you continue your visit at Swann Hall if the company does not please you. Mr. Swann mentioned yesterday that you were on your way to your hunting box. It is close by, I believe?"

"To tell the truth, I always enjoy a good family squabble. Having stumbled into a prime one, I am loath to leave until it is settled, one way or the other—by trick or by treaty."

"It *is* settled, Lord Fenwick. My aunt was legally married. She is Pargeter's heir. Or does Lady Sykes plan to take the matter to court?"

"I believe I've talked her out of that folly. You can thank me later. But if you think the matter is settled, ma'am, I take leave to tell you, you are hopelessly naive. It has only begun. There is an exceedingly wealthy widow and her charming niece to be married off, preferably to obliging relatives of Lady Sykes."

She stared in confusion. "I expect Aunt Fay will receive offers, but I am not wealthy. I'm a working lady, and in my experience, poverty has always proved a sovereign prevention against marriage."

"But you are speaking of arranged marriages," he pointed out. "Your modern lad and lass have been known to flout common sense and marry where their hearts dictate, with the somewhat dim-witted notion of living on love."

"With the cold pudding of poverty for dessert."

"No, no! You were supposed to disagree with that cynical 'dimwitted,' Miss Lonsdale. How can we enjoy a good argument if you go agreeing with my antique notions? It is your duty as a penniless orphan to push for marriages of love. A cat may look at a king, and a dowerless lady may hope for an offer from a prince."

"The only offer I look forward to is one of employment, if Fay does marry, that is. Certainly she would not do so in the near future. She's still in mourning."

Fenwick cocked his head to one side and directed a knowing look at her. "Well, if you insist on talking common sense, mourning did not prove a deterrent against marriage for your aunt—nor did poverty, come to that. I believe it is Lady Pargeter I should be having this conversation with."

"There were special circumstances," Jane pointed out.

Having lulled her suspicions by his nonsense, Fenwick began to work the conversation around to Miss Prism's Academy, hoping to learn Miss Lonsdale's secret, for he felt there was some secret lurking there. Whether it was her illegitimacy or a matter relating to misdoing on her own part, he was curious to discover.

"Do you miss your students, Miss Lonsdale?" he asked.

"One always has a few pets, but in general, I own I am happier here than at the academy."

"I expect it would actually be the other schoolmistresses you were closer to."

"Yes, I had one particular friend, Harriet Stowe. Our backgrounds were rather similar. Both clergymen's daughters. Harriet was in worse case than I. She had no relatives when her papa died."

"She was fortunate to have been hired by Miss Prism. I believe one requires some connections to be taken on there?"

She noticed the keen eye with which he regarded her, and was suddenly suspicious. "I had no special connections. I believe that, like myself, her papa knew some influential clergyman in Bath."

"And is that all that's required? One would think the line of hopeful applicants would be a mile long.

I thought perhaps Lord Pargeter put in a word for you."

"No, how should he? I didn't know him at the time."

"You didn't visit your aunt at Wildercliffe before this visit?"

"Yes, once when the first Lady Pargeter was still alive."

"You got on well with Pargeter?"

"I scarcely met him. And that was *after* I was working at the academy, Lord Fenwick. I assure you he had nothing to do with my being hired." She could find no reason for his questions. He had been listening when Lady Sykes covered the same ground earlier. This conversation seemed pointless, unless he felt she was unqualified as a schoolmistress. "I was hired for my talents," she said stiffly.

"I'm sure they are formidable, Miss Lonsdale."

She stared at him a moment before speaking, trying to gauge his intention. He met her gaze, but she read some guile in his expression. He smiled, but it was an insincere smile.

"No, they are only average. Formidable talents are not required to teach young ladies reading and writing."

"Of course." Fenwick nodded. "Character, I expect, is of equal or even more importance."

Her tongue touched her lips nervously. "Quite," she said.

Fenwick's interest soared, but before he could pursue this new line of inquiry, Swann was upon them. He used his empty cup as an excuse to escape Lady Sykes. When he had filled his cup, he joined Fenwick and Jane.

"Pity our outing was canceled, Miss Lonsdale," he said. "We shall do it tomorrow, if you like."

"I look forward to it," she replied. Relief showed on every line of her face, and Fenwick was sharp enough to see it. She was definitely uncomfortable discussing character. He was intrigued that such an innocent-seeming lady should harbor a secret vice. What could it be?

"I must visit Wilkie and Minerva this afternoon, rain or no," Swann continued. "They only hatched six eggs this year. They usually hatch seven. With only the one breeding pair left, I can take no chances. I am on the lookout for a pair of black swans. You wouldn't happen to know of a pair for sale?"

"I've never even seen a black one," she told him.

"Some neighbors of mine in Surrey have a pair, but I doubt they would part with them," Fenwick mentioned.

Swann sipped his tea and glanced about the room. "Old Horace is acting pretty coy," he said. "Trying his luck with Miss—with Lady Pargeter. Hard to remember to give her her title when she has been Miss Rampling forever. Phoebe will never bring it off."

Jane continued drinking her tea, but Fenwick caught her eye and smiled.

"If worst comes to worst, Miss Lonsdale, I know several families who would be happy to hire a governess with experience at Miss Prism's Seminary," he said in a joking way.

"What the deuce are you talking about?" Swann asked angrily. "Miss Lonsdale ain't looking for a position. She just got here. She has not even seen my swans yet."

"I was discussing future possibilities, after Miss Lonsdale has seen your swans," he said.

The visit did not last long. As soon as the tea was finished, the callers left.

While they were driving home, Phoebe said, "The chit is certainly Pargeter's by-blow. I noticed a marked resemblance, but I shall not call Nigel until it is settled that she is to inherit Wildercliffe, or he will go falling in love with her, for she is a little prettier than I had expected."

Fenwick had seen no such resemblance. Jane's conversation told him she had no thought of inheriting, yet she had become quite vexed when he harped on her former acquaintance with Pargeter. There was some mystery there, some irregularity.

He stifled a yawn and said, "Surely love is a prerequisite for marriage, Phoebe."

"What bizarre notions you modern fellows harbor. Love is fatal to a happy marriage. It produces nothing but jealousy and arguments. Your mama would stare to hear you speak so foolishly, Fenwick. Love indeed! I shall invite them to Swann Hall for dinner, to forward the relationship."

"It's my house," Swann said, his ire rising.

"Indeed it is, and I want you to do the thing up nicely, Scawen. Two or three courses and as many removes. You must not mention it to your mama, or she will want to join the party. She'll ruin it, with her dribbling and meandering talk. What a trial it is when the old folks don't know enough to die. Did you notice the housekeeper was wearing Lizzie's pearls, Fenwick? I wonder if the jewelry was left to her outright in the will. It is worth fifty thousand easily. The Pargeter diamonds alone must be worth close to twenty thousand."

"Ten," Scawen said.

Phoebe ignored him. She was the sort of lady who dealt in hyperbole. Her enemies were all blackguards, and her few friends were saints. Anyone with five thousand a year was a nabob, and anyone with less than five was a pauper.

"See if you can find out the next time you call, Horace," she said. "But do it discreetly. You did very well, by the by. I knew someone of your cut would just suit the housekeeper."

At Wildercliffe, the visit was also being discussed.

"Lady Sykes plans to palm that disreputable brother of hers off on me," Lady Pargeter said, and laughed merrily. "She must think I'm easy to please, if I would marry that sponge. What had Fenwick to say, Jane?"

"He mentioned the same possibility," she said.

"I begin to see why they came. There is one good thing in it at least. It seems Lady Sykes has decided not to go to court. I would dislike the bother. Shall we have a snack before lunch? I am feeling peckish."

"You go ahead. I'm not hungry, after sitting all morning. You'll be putting on weight if you keep up at this rate, Aunt Fay."

Lady Pargeter called for bread and butter and some cold mutton, promising she would go out and walk as soon as the rain let up. Jane sat on, mentally reviewing her first flirtation, and wondering if it had been a flirtation, or merely a diversion to cover an interrogation. Lord Fenwick had asked a dozen seemingly pointless questions. Why did he think Pargeter had taken an interest in her? He had something in mind, but for the life of her, she couldn't fathom what it was.

Chapter Seven

The next morning dawned fair. From his study window, Lord Malton saw the sun glinting on newly leafed trees, fresh from the spring rain. A light breeze stirred their branches. On an impulse he rose and threw open the mullioned window, a thing he seldom did. As a warm zephyr blew over him, he felt some long-forgotten stirrings of life. It was Fenwick's recent visit that called to mind his late friend Pargeter, and his widow. A fine-looking woman, Rampling. He had always thought so. Many a time he and Pargeter had regretted her being a lady. On an impulse, Lord Malton decided to call for his carriage and pay a call on Lady Pargeter.

He took a glance at himself in the gilt-framed mirror in the entrance hallway as he left, and gave a shudder of distaste. Where had this old man come from? His nice tawny mane of hair had faded to gray decades ago, and had nearly left his head entirely over the past ten years. The tawny hair would have looked like the devil with his ruddy nose and cheeks, but he wished he had more than a fringe of white to cover his pate. His stomach preceded him by half a foot, but by God, he still looked like a gentleman. He had not begun drooling on his waistcoat, and he could walk with the brisk step of a fifty-year-old.

Lady Pargeter was quite simply amazed to receive a call from him half an hour later. He had always treated her with a certain avuncular jollity that was half flirtation and half genuine friendship. She soon saw that his manner had not changed in the least.

"Lady Pargeter! I trust this old ghost from the past does not frighten you," he said, walking forward and raising her hand to his lips.

"Lord Malton! I couldn't be more surprised if you were a ghost." His smile told Fay that the call was a friendly one. "Why have you been ignoring me?" she demanded.

"Because I'm a lazy hound, and could not drag myself out of the house in winter. It was Lord Fenwick's call t'other day that brought you to mind. Not that I had forgotten you entirely! At my age, you must know, I'd forget to eat my dinner if the servants didn't call me. Oh, I am a sad wreck of humanity. A sad creature. May I have a glass of wine?"

"You were not used to be so formal, Lord Malton. Help yourself."

"Don't you think you might dispense with the 'Lord' after all these years, Ramp—Lady Pargeter?" He stopped and shook his head. "No, I cannot call you by that name. Lizzie will always be Lady Pargeter to me. You are Rampling, but as it wouldn't do to call you so now, I shall call you Fay," he said daringly.

He poured the wine and they settled in for a good coze.

"Young Fenwick was sniffing around to see what

he could discover," he said. "Sykes put him up to it, no doubt."

"You didn't tell him?"

"Not the whole, until we see how things come out. Mind you, you can't keep it a secret forever."

"There's plenty of time. Did Fenwick tell you my niece is staying with me?"

"He mentioned it. Where is she?"

"Swann has taken her to see his swans."

"Ah, Swann," he said fondly. "You ought to encourage her to have him. An excellent fellow, Swann. He'll never nab a wife on his own. Swann Hall needs a lady's touch. Poor old Mrs. Swann is past it. I hear she's completely bed-bound. How cruel time is. I remember her as a pretty lady when I was in short coats. She was quite the belle of the parish."

Lord Malton remained for an hour, chatting and enjoying the little flirtation immensely. When he left, his step was lighter, almost youthful.

At Swann Lake, Jane Lonsdale was also enjoying her morning. She had been pleasantly surprised to see that Lord Fenwick accompanied Swann when he called for her. He was dressed more casually on this occasion, with a dotted Belcher kerchief in lieu of a cravat, but wearing the same blue jacket, which hugged his broad, straight shoulders. His chestnut hair, brushed forward in the stylish Brutus do, gleamed in the sunlight. Swann could not have chosen a companion more likely to cast him in the shade.

"I talked Fenwick into coming with us," Swann said. "The swans can be a trifle testy when they have their young about."

"It didn't take much persuasion," Fenwick said to Jane, with a warm smile. "I had planned to horn in on the visit, and was saved the ignominy of begging."

She sensed a new interest in his attentions. He looked at her in a certain way. It was hard to put a finger on, but his eyes seemed warmer, more interested in her as a woman. Best of all, he didn't badger her with questions.

They all walked together with the brilliant spring sunshine warming their shoulders. They did not skirt the meadow, but cut through it to the far, narrow end of the crescent lake near Swann Hall, where the swans nested. Walking was difficult through the tall grass, but neither gentleman offered Jane an arm. She enjoyed the luxury of being out in such fine weather, with two gentlemen escorts, and not a single thought of having to hurry back to prepare lessons or mark essays. A feeling of freedom possessed her. It required the greatest effort to restrain herself from running through the flower-spangled meadow. She could not resist the impulse to lift her face to the sun and feel its warmth caressing her. How lovely life was!

Fenwick watched her bemusedly. He didn't speak, but he felt touched by her enjoyment of such a simple outing. What sort of life did a schoolmistress lead? He had never had occasion to consider it, but he found himself considering it now, and he felt a pang of pity for Miss Lonsdale, and all the ladies like her.

"Take care or you'll get freckles," Swann cautioned, when he saw what she was doing.

"I don't care if I do," she answered, and laughed in pure pleasure of her freedom.

"Nor do I," Swann said. "I like freckles. The nest is just along here," he added, leading her toward the lake. "Swans mate for life. They might use the nest again, or build a new one next year if they feel like it."

She saw a rather disorganized heap of vegetation. "Oh, I thought it would be neater, like a robin's nest, only larger."

"No, it's a bit of a mess. You can see some of the broken eggs. They shoved the shells out of the nest." Pale shards of broken eggs lay on the ground.

"Where are the swans?" she asked.

"I fancy they're feeding. They eat the greenery that grows along the lake's edge, and plants that grow in the shallow water. That is why they're always putting their heads in the water. They ain't trying to drown themselves, as I used to think when I was a lad."

They went to the edge of the lake, but saw no sign of the birds. As they watched, a graceful swan sailed forth from the rushes. The bird floated for a few yards, then ducked its head under the water, searching for food.

"Is that the mother?" Jane asked.

"Pen—the female is called a pen," Swann said. "The male is a cob. It's hard to tell them apart; there's no difference in the plumage, but Wilkie is the larger. If they was together, you could tell which was which."

As they watched, the swan floated toward them. It left the water and waddled up onto dry land to begin nibbling on grass.

"A comical walk, they have," Swann said. "The black bit around the eyes and top of the beak make them look angry. We'll go down the shore a bit. T'other one must be hiding in the rushes."

Another swan sailed forth, carrying six little clumps of brownish-white down on her back. "Oh, how sweet!" Jane exclaimed. "Can the cygnets not swim?"

"They can. The cob pushes them into the water when they're a day old, but they tire easily and hitch a ride from Minerva. That must be Minerva. Wilkie don't give free rides."

"Just like a man!" Jane said pertly.

"Why, I'm sure I would be happy to give you a ride any time, Miss Lonsdale," Swann said. "Only not on my back, of course. Heh heh. I'm not a cob, after all. That is to say—"

Jane noticed Lord Fenwick's lips move unsteadily. "And I am not a cygnet," she said. "I know what you mean, Mr. Swann."

"So, is it a date?"

"What do you mean?"

"Give you a hurl in my carriage?"

"Oh, that would be nice."

"Bibury. I shall drive you to Bibury very soon. Go on the strut on the High Street. Have a look at the church. You can go shopping, if you like. I've no objection to poking through the shops."

Fenwick glanced at Jane again, expecting to share a smile at this simple outing. He was surprised to see her genuine pleasure.

She was thinking what a kind man Swann was. "I should like it very much, Mr. Swann," she said.

"Good. All settled, then. Now, let us have a closer look at Minerva and her brood. Ah, here she comes now. Daresay she is tired out from carrying her family on her back."

Minerva sailed closer. At the same time, Swann took a step toward her, with Jane following. Jane put out her hand to pick up one of the downy cygnets as they came ashore.

At once, Wilkie came charging toward them, wings raised in a threatening pose and his head down. The swan, usually silent, gave an angry barking sound as it advanced. He made a dart at Jane's skirts. The graceful bird looked much larger with his wings spread. As she turned to flee, the cob snatched the bottom of her skirt in his beak and began pulling at it.

She shouted, more in alarm than fear, though her heart was pounding. Fenwick picked up a fallen branch and made feinting passes at the bird, while Swann grabbed Jane's hand and pulled her away. Wilkie released her skirt and subsided somewhat, but kept his wings raised in a menacing attitude, ready to attack again.

Jane was trembling. She noticed Fenwick took a step forward, as if to comfort her. Then he looked at Swann and came to a stop, although Swann made no effort to comfort her.

She said, "I have heard swans are bad tempered, but I've never seen one in a pelter before."

"You shouldn't have reached for the cygnet," Swann told her. "I ought to have warned you."

"I should have known. Any animal will attack when it feels its young are threatened. Even a robin, or a blackbird. How brave they are."

They watched from a distance as both mature swans began pulling at the grass surrounding the lake. Fenwick noticed that the grass was nearly all gone.

"You had two dozen swans last year, did you say?" he asked Scawen.

"Aye, and now I'm down to four, along with the chicks. First they moved to the far end of the lake, then they disappeared entirely."

"Two dozen is a large flock for this small area," Fenwick said, glancing around. "I wonder if they didn't clear out the food supply. You should put out some grain for them. Birds won't stay where they can't feed."

"I shall speak to the gardener at once. He looks after the swans," Scawen said, frowning at the frazzled remains of grass. "And while we're at the Hall, I shall get Miss Lonsdale a glass of wine. She is pale as paper. Let us go along. Mama looks forward to meeting you, Miss Lonsdale."

With a thought of Lady Sykes, Jane preferred to return to Wildercliffe.

"I look a fright, Mr. Swann. I wore my oldest gown and these old shoes. My shoes are wet and now my skirt is muddied from Wilkie. Another time."

"Mama won't mind. She always looks a fright." He looked at his swans, and decided they were starving to death.

"I would really rather not," Jane said again.

"Then we must get you home at once." Again he looked at the hungry swans and frowned. Their topaz eyes seemed to be demanding nourishment.

"I can take Miss Lonsdale home, if you're in a hurry to speak to Jenkins," Fenwick offered.

"If you're sure you don't mind," Swann said.

"It would be a pleasure," Fenwick assured him.

Swann hurried off to speak to Jenkins, and Fenwick offered Jane his arm for the return trip.

She felt a little shy, with Fenwick's hand holding her elbow.

"It was an interesting outing, even if I did dirty my gown," she said. "I've never had close contact with swans before. They looked so harmless and beautiful, floating on the Avon in Bath. I shall never look at them in quite the same way again. It was foolish of me to try to pick up the cygnet."

Fenwick stopped walking and looked down at her. "You are a wonder, Miss Lonsdale. Most ladies would be fainting and carping and complaining. I see you're going to be easy to entertain."

She looked quite shocked at the notion of Lord Fenwick entertaining her. "I am accustomed to entertaining myself."

This statement also struck him as a wonder. Young ladies did not usually dismiss his offers of friendship so cavalierly. "And how does Miss Lonsdale usually entertain Miss Lonsdale?" he inquired, with growing interest.

They resumed their stroll through the meadow. "Miss Lonsdale finds herself easy to entertain. Reading novels, looking at the shop windows, visiting with her friends."

It was the words "looking at shop windows" that called up a pathetic image of Miss Lonsdale with her pretty nose pressed against the pane, ogling all the elegant trifles she couldn't afford. He sensed, however, that she would disdain pity.

"And here I have been pitying schoolmistresses," he said jokingly. "Why, your life is a virtual round of gaiety. It seems you have come to the right place to continue it. Do you ride, Miss Lonsdale?"

"I had an old cob when I was younger. An equine cob," she added, with a smile.

"So I gathered. You've already mentioned your lack of familiarity with swans. I brought my hacker with me. Scawen has a couple of mounts in his stable. Perhaps the three of us can go riding one day." He did not particularly want to include Swann in their ride. He wanted to become better acquainted with this quaint little lady, but he felt it would be underhanded to cut Scawen out.

"That would be lovely. Such a lot to do, and here I thought it would be lonesome at Wildercliffe."

Again Fenwick felt that wince of pity. "And there is still church on Sunday to add to the merriment. You will be hard-pressed to fit Lady Sykes's dinner party into your schedule."

She turned a startled face to him. Her long eyelashes fluttered a moment. "Is she having a party? I doubt she will invite Aunt Fay and me."

"You are mistaken. The party is in your honor."

She gave him a doubting look. "That is certainly a change."

"Phoebe is not one to follow a fruitless course forever."

"No invitation had been delivered when we left the house, but if it comes, I cannot promise my aunt will accept. You must have noticed the two were at daggers drawn yesterday."

"It promises to be an—interesting evening. I know you will try to convince your aunt to accept."

"How do you know that?"

They came to a stream, really just a shallow ditch with water lying an inch deep. Fenwick's long legs stepped across with no trouble, but Jane hesitated. He gave her his hand to assist her. She daintily lifted her skirts and jumped across. They didn't continue walking immediately.

Fenwick looked at her upturned face, with the sunlight streaming on it. The sun glinted on her brown curls, gilding them in gold. He wondered if those pink patches on her cheeks were due to the fresh air, or pleasure in her outing. What a pretty little thing she was, in her own quiet way.

"You said yesterday you wished the ladies could be friendly," he reminded her.

"Yes, but that was before I had seen them together. It promises to be a horrid evening, if my aunt does accept."

"Family gatherings are usually horrid, one way or the other," he said, and smiled ruefully at the memory of large family gatherings he had attended.

"Really?" She frowned to consider this. "I always regretted having so few relatives. My friends used to have their houses bulging at Christmas, with aunts and cousins and I don't know what all. At home there was just Papa and myself. I don't remember Mama at all. She died when I was born."

Fenwick murmured some sympathetic sound. He was thinking that if Pargeter had put his by-blow up for adoption, he would not have left her with a widower. He would have put her in a home with a mother.

"Family parties combine the worst of all worlds," he said. "Intimacy and familiarity without the civility we accord to outsiders. You will see what I mean at Phoebe's dinner party."

"That doesn't encourage me to urge Auntie to attend." Yet she wanted to go. Fenwick and Swann would be there. "Swann will make it a pleasant evening," she said.

Fenwick felt a jolt of annoyance. "Fenwick will

also do his poor best to make the evening pleasant," he said. Then he took her hand and continued the walk.

First she had repelled his offer of friendship, and now she had compared him unfavorably to Swann. Why was Miss Lonsdale immune to him? The little puzzle gnawed at him after he had seen her home. Miss Lonsdale was certainly different from the other ladies he met. She was more provincial, with virtually no experience of gentlemen. He was not unduly conceited, but experience told him she ought to be bowled over by his wealth and title, if not his person. Yet she preferred Scawen Swann. It was a baffling situation.

Having decided there was no scandal in Miss Lonsdale's past—she was a vicar's daughter who had got her position at Miss Prism's through ecclesiastical connections—he was now faced with another mystery. Why did a pretty young lady not throw her bonnet at the most eligible gentleman she had ever met? Had she no ambition to better herself? Her aunt's success must have shown her such a thing was possible. Had she no romance in her soul? Impossible! She might have stepped right out of one of those novels ladies read: a poor, beautiful orphan, working for a living. Why didn't she recognize her hero when he was right under her nose?

Chapter Eight

When Jane returned to Wildercliffe, Lady Pargeter informed her of Lord Malton's call.

"He behaved just like his old self, as friendly as can stare," Fay said. "It was not Lady Skykes's interference that has kept him away, but age and indolence. It was good to see the old rogue again. He promised he would come back soon. I doubt he will come, but at least I know he is on my side. And how was your outing, Jane?"

"Wilkie attacked us," she said, and told the story of the cob.

"Nasty things, swans. I cannot imagine why all the world admires them so. One of them made a flying start at me the last time I went down to the lake for a stroll. It frightened the life out of me. You and Scawen get along well, do you?" she asked, and looked sharply for a reaction.

Everyone liked Swann. It had occurred to Lady Pargeter even before sending for her niece that Jane might like him well enough to marry him. It would be nice to have Jane living close by. It was even nicer to have her at Wildercliffe, but she must not be selfish. Jane was young, and should look out for her future. Fay would not live forever.

"I like him very much. He's so foolish, and so

easy to talk to. I never feel uncomfortable with him, as I do with Lord Fenwick."

"Oh, Fenwick! He's a handsome rogue, but I wouldn't waste any time throwing my hankie at him. All the fine ladies are after Fenwick. That would be looking a good deal too high."

Jane colored up briskly. "I have no intention of throwing my bonnet at him. Such a thought never entered my head." Yet she felt guilty. It was impossible to meet someone like Lord Fenwick and not at least wonder what it would be like to be a part of his world. To change the subject, she mentioned that Lady Sykes was planning to invite them to a dinner party.

This news was received with disbelief, tinged with suspicion. "It's a hoax. If she is inviting me to dinner, it is only in the hope of poisoning me."

"I think it's an olive branch, Aunt Fay. You want to reestablish yourself in the neighborhood. Why refuse this first offer?"

"I'd like to know what the shrew is up to," Lady Pargeter said. "First calling, now asking us to dinner. That is one gift horse whose mouth I shall examine thoroughly before accepting. She couldn't have known of Malton's call so soon."

"You mentioned inviting the folks from Swann Hall to dinner. No doubt Lady Sykes had a similar idea."

"I shall go, and I shall wear the Pargeter diamonds to rile her," she said, and laughed spitefully.

Jane began to see that family parties could be every bit as disconcerting as Fenwick had said.

In the afternoon Lady Pargeter had another nap. Jane donned an ill-fitting riding habit five years old and went to the stable to see if there was a suitable mount. She was not a very experienced rider, but she enjoyed the sport. The groom recommended Brownie, a middle-aged bay mare of mild disposition, and accompanied her on a ride about the estate to familiarize her with the animal. She enjoyed her outing immensely, and thought that if Fenwick happened to invite her out riding, she could now acquit herself without shame.

When she returned, Fay was having an early tea with Lord Malton, who had been to see his man of business in Bibury, and brought her the latest journals. The two of them were obviously on friendly terms. In fact, Lord Malton's behavior was not an inch short of flirtation. He seemed unhappy with Jane's return, and left almost at once.

"Your new beau is wasting no time," Jane said.

"He's lonesome, as I was myself, before you came," Fay replied.

"All this eating and no exercise!" Jane scolded when she saw the cold mutton and bread, the plum cake and other dainties spread out. "Tomorrow you and I are going for a long walk in the park." Then, after scolding her aunt, she partook of a substantial tea herself. The teas at Miss Prism's had been parsimonious in the extreme. And besides, her ride had whetted her appetite.

The remainder of the afternoon passed quietly. Jane found some old fashion magazines and looked through them for a pattern for a riding habit. With her new salary, she could afford to splurge. It was not the undemanding Swann she had in mind when she chose her pattern and mentally selected a royal blue serge for the material. It was Lord

Fenwick. She shook away the thought. Fenwick wouldn't even be here by the time the habit was made up. He would be continuing to his hunting box any day now, thence back to London, or Brighton, or to his estate.

The ladies dressed for dinner, which reminded Jane she would also have to have a few evening gowns made up. She would not choose black, but subdued colors that honored Lord Pargeter's passing without actually going into mourning for this gentleman she had met only once.

When the door knocker sounded at eight-thirty, she was sitting with her aunt, discussing her new gowns. Fay had not begrudged the cost of mourning, and she had not settled for bombazine either. She wore a black crape gown and again the pearls. Jane wore a modest navy lutestring gown that was used on those rare occasions when evening wear was required at Miss Prism's. Miss Grundy herself could have found no fault in its neckline, which revealed no more than the clavicle. The sleeves came to just below the elbow. Miss Prism did not approve of her schoolmistresses flaunting their charms. She insisted they all wear similar navy gowns and identical white muslin caps. The outfits robbed them of their individuality.

Both ladies looked lively at the sound of masculine voices from the hall. Broome soon appeared at the doorway to announce Lord Fenwick, Messrs. Swann and Gurney. Gurney made a dash toward Lady Pargeter and the wine decanter. Jane, in a turbulence of happy confusion, was left to entertain the younger gentlemen. She felt her eyes turning more than once to admire Lord Fenwick's elegant black evening suit. A diamond of just the right size, neither ostentatiously large nor meagerly small, twinkled in the folds of his immaculate cravat. She tore her eyes away to examine Scawen, who looked, as usual, like an unmade bed. The black of his jacket was liberally sprinkled with dust. His cowlick rose like a jay's crest at the back of his head. He had nicked his chin while shaving, and not bothered to remove the daub of powder he had put on to stanch the flow of blood.

It was Swann who delivered the dinner invitations. Lady Sykes, always a high stickler for the proprieties, had written up separate cards for the two ladies. Jane read hers and looked to her aunt for guidance.

"Thank you, Scawen," Lady Pargeter said, setting the card aside. "It happens Jane and I are free tomorrow evening. We shall be happy to attend."

"Not really a party," Scawen said apologetically. "Just ourselves and one or two neighbors."

"Then we need not write a formal reply. You will tell Lady Sykes."

"Told her she need not write cards. But that is Phoebe all over. She actually enjoys writing cards and letters." He shook his head in wonder, his cowlick wobbling.

Jane girded herself to do the pretty by her guests. "Did you arrange with your gardener to put extra food out for the swans?" she asked Scawen.

"I did, and they went at it as if they were starving, poor souls. It is as Fenwick said, the large flock ate up all the water plants. Now that we are down to the smaller number, the plants will grow back. The lake can't accommodate two dozen. I aim at one dozen even. Once the grass grows back, I shall buy a pair of black swans."

The swans having been discussed, she rooted around for something to say to Fenwick. Her life at Bath had been so narrow that she couldn't think of a thing. She did not attend plays or balls, routs or concerts. She knew none of his friends. He wouldn't be interested to hear Miss Prism was raising her charge to parents, but not raising her teachers' salaries accordingly. That and Fortini's unwanted advances had been the main items of interest in her life for the past month. After ten minutes' uneasy conversation about how she was enjoying life in the country, Lord Fenwick came to the rescue.

"Do you play the pianoforte, Miss Lonsdale?" he asked.

"A little. I'm a bit rusty, I fear."

"Then you didn't teach music at Miss Prism's?"

"No, we had a music master who came in twice a week," she said. Her eyes glittered and a light flush suffused her cheeks at the mention of Fortini.

Fenwick noticed her animation, and wondered at it. Had there been a romance between the two? "I expect the music master caused quite a flurry in the dovecote," he said.

"No! Why do you say that?" she asked in alarm.

"They have a reputation that way. Did I touch a nerve?" he asked archly.

"No, not at all," she said firmly, but the color in her cheeks heightened noticeably.

"If you'd care to give the piano a try, Fenwick and me will sing," Scawen said. "I know all the words to 'Green Grow the Rushes, Ho' and the chorus of 'The

Maid of Lodi.' Mind you, my pipes are a bit rusty as well, but I'm game to give her a try."

Jane cast a grateful little smile on her rescuer and rose at once. They went to the Music Room, a stately chamber that held a hundred seats arranged as in a theater. The walls were embossed and the ceiling was painted to resemble the sky, with cherubs frolicking amidst the clouds. The pianoforte sat on a raised platform. The late Lord Pargeter had enjoyed music, and often held musical soirees. There were also a clavichord and two harps on the platform.

"This is rather intimidating," Jane said, gazing around at the large room as she took her place at the piano bench.

"At least there's no one but ourselves to hear if we hit a sour note," Swann said.

Jane played a few tunes and the gentlemen sang. She enjoyed Fenwick's firm baritone. Swann sang surprisingly well, too, but the interlude was strained. Her playing was indeed rusty, and with Fenwick standing at her shoulder, her fingers refused to behave themselves. It was not a room for intimate music. The notes seemed to echo like ghosts from the high rafters and bounce mischievously from the walls and windows.

"It's those empty chairs that defeat us," Fenwick said, after the second song.

"Thank God they ain't full," Scawen added.

"I know how the actors of a poorly attended play feel now. Unappreciated, unwanted, and soon unemployed. Let us go," Jane said, glad to have it over and done with.

"I expect you've been perusing the library," Fenwick said to Jane as they left the room. She had claimed an interest in books. He had observed her lack of ease, and wished to strike some subject that interested her. He was rewarded with the first real smile he had seen all evening. Her lips had an enchanting way of trembling when she was happy, almost as if she feared her moment of pleasure would be snatched away from her.

"Yes indeed. My favorite room. It's a wonderful library, but not quite up-to-date. I fear the late Lady Pargeter was not one for novels. I can find nothing by Edgeworth or Fanny Burney."

"Now, there is a project to fill your idle hours— bringing the library up-to-date," he said. "Let us go and see what is missing."

Scawen disliked books nearly as much as he disliked large parties and overbearing females. He accompanied them to the library, another room as big as a barn, with racks of books running up to the ceiling, and marble busts of old writers glaring superciliously from their perches atop pedestals.

As the talk was all of books, he soon said, "I shall just nip back and see how Lady Pargeter goes on." What he meant was that the tea tray might be there by now, but he disliked to reveal his keen interest in tea and plum cake.

"You have a deal of buying to do, Miss Lonsdale," Fenwick said, perusing the shelves that held novels. "There is nothing here from this century, not even the Walter Scott novels. Posterity will condemn your aunt; they will have no first editions to sell when they run into dun territory. Have you tried Scott?"

"Yes, I didn't care for him," she said.

Fenwick stared. "You're out of step with the rest of the nation. What did not please you?"

"They were too full of wonders for me. Like Lord Byron—I cannot warm to him either."

"That is literary heresy of a high order, ma'am, to denigrate our top-ranking novelist and poet. Next you will claim to dislike roast beef, and I shall know you are a rebel."

"I'm quite fond of roast beef, I assure you."

"What writers do you like?" He listened with interest, rather surprised at this modest lady's daring to express an original opinion. Oh dear! Her prim lips told him she was going to say Hannah More, that sanctimonious purveyor of religiosity.

"More down-to-earth stories, with real-seeming people. I cannot relate to the corsairs and banditti and self-indulgent heroes, wallowing in their vague guilt, that Byron gives us, nor to the kidnapping and smugglers and gypsies of *Guy Mannering*. They are too far from anything I've known in life."

"Yet it is hard to capture a reader's interest with writing in which nothing exciting happens."

"I prefer Mrs. Edgeworth, and Fanny Burney. For lighter reading, I like Mrs. Radcliffe. Just for a diversion, you know, at the end of a hard day's work," she said apologetically.

Fenwick gave her a teasing smile. "You prefer the more down-to-earth trials of Emily de St. Aubert, I see. An orphan, a wicked guardian, kidnapping; the appurtenances of melodrama are all right, so long as they center around a young lady. I take leave to tell you, Miss Lonsdale, you are a fraud. You are shamming it. You like exactly the same sort of nonsense I like myself. Your only preference is that a lady be the main character of the tale."

Jane gave him a sly smile. "I see you are familiar with Mrs. Radcliffe as well, milord."

"I love her—and unlike some, I don't hesitate to admit my vulgar taste. We all enjoy that vicarious sense of adventure and romance that is missing in our own lives."

"I cannot think romance is missing in your life!" she exclaimed, before she had time to get a rein on her tongue.

Fenwick's eyebrows lifted in surprise. He had not thought Miss Lonsdale would be so forthcoming. He saw he had been keeping a bothersome and needless guard on his tongue. The evening promised not to be a dead loss after all.

"Oh, romance! I know plenty of ladies, but no put-upon orphans or interesting kidnap victims. My friends are all demmed ordinary when you come down to it. You are the only lady worthy of the name heroine I have ever met."

"Me?" she asked, staring as if he had run mad, then she laughed. "Oh, you are funning, milord. I am as ordinary as suet pudding."

"No, a good deal more—appetizing. I believe you have a few romances up your sleeve as well?" He directed a brightly quizzical look at her.

She blinked in astonishment. "No, not one. Wherever did you get that notion?"

"Despite your quick denial—or perhaps because of it—I suspect the music master. I noticed a certain sparkle in your eye when he was mentioned. A rosy flush suffusing your cheek—quite in the style of Mademoiselle de St. Aubert," he said playfully. The same manifestations of excitement were on her face now, adding charm to her modest beauty.

"Oh no, there was nothing in that!" she exclaimed, and blushed as red as a rose. She immediately rushed away from the subject. "I thought you meant Scawen Swann. He has asked me out a few times, and now this dinner party . . ."

"He finds you 'dashed pretty,' but you've got hold of the wrong end of the stick regarding the dinner party. It is not Scawen who is courting you there. It is Lady Sykes, on behalf of her son, Nigel."

"Why would she do that? I have no dowry."

Fenwick bit his lips to keep them steady. It was unusual to hear the truth expressed so bluntly. "And they call you a clever minx! Your wits are gone begging, Miss Lonsdale."

"What is amiss with him?" she asked suspiciously. "Is he a moonling, or hideously deformed?"

"Not *hideously*, no. And not quite a moonling either. He could find a lady to have him, I think. But you are Lady Pargeter's only living relative. You will outlive her by a decade or two. You're bound to come into a tidy fortune."

Jane laughed aloud. "Talk about a pig in a poke. Who is to say Fay will not marry herself? She is still youngish."

"As Scawen would be the first to tell you, a lady cannot marry herself."

"No, but she can marry a gentleman—say, Lord Malton. He has been calling recently."

"Lord Malton!" His brow furrowed in surprise. "Is that the way the wind blows?"

"There is no saying. He is an excellent oiler. Gurney doesn't hold a candle to him in the butter department."

"Aha! The plot thickens. We now have that romantic figure beloved by gossips and mathematicians, the amorous triangle. And another triangle as well."

She cocked her head to one side and looked at him. "What is this second triangle?"

He waggled a well-shaped finger and perched on the end of the table, settling in for a flirtation. "For shame, Miss Lonsdale, and you call yourself a schoolmistress. Or at least Lady Sykes calls you one—endlessly. I mean your charming self, Nigel, and Scawen. We ought to be able to make up some sort of theorem out of all this material. Let me see, now, the square on the hypotenuse of a right-angled— No, that requires a triangle and a square. We are short an angle. Ah, I have it. It is a deduction we are looking at here, not a theorem. What we must prove is that—"

"The matter requires no deducing. It is simple arithmetic we are dealing with, for it is plain as the nose on your face—and that, if you do not mind my saying so, milord, is very plain—that two fortune hunters cannot be divided into one fortune." Jane's color heightened at the brashness of her reply. Had she really accused Fenwick of having a big nose? It was too ridiculous—his nose was perfect. She meant it in a metaphorical sense, for he did seem to be encroaching into very personal matters. He revealed no offense, however, but only gave her a bold smile.

"Well, not without committing bigamy," he allowed.

"I believe we can rule that out. The fortune is my aunt's."

"I assume you don't teach higher mathematics, ma'am? Two can be divided into one. The result is one half. One half of fifty thousand is twenty-five thousand, and a very respectable sum it is, too. A lady with twenty-five thousand might make a pitch

86

for a duke without overreaching herself. Nigel will not thumb his nose at it. And by the by, that remark about my nose was unkind and gratuitous."

"Quite uncalled-for, and I do apologize." Then she peered up at him through her lashes and added daringly, "Your nose is not out of keeping with the size of your head."

He gave a mock scowl. "And my heart. I forgive you for yet another gratuitous slur on my person. A big head indeed! There is no offending me, you see. Like the hound I am, I thrive on injury. Watch out, or you will add another point to your triangle and have a square on your hands. Then we can get on with the Pythagorean theorem."

Scawen came ambling in. "Square on the right triangle of the hypotenuse angle—something of the sort. Why the devil are you badgering Miss Lonsdale with algebra, Fenwick? Or is it geometry? No matter. You are boring the poor girl to tears."

Fenwick turned a laughing eye on Jane, who had never been less bored in her life, and looked it. "Brave little woman that she is, I see she is laughing through her tears."

"Are you always so ridiculous, Lord Fenwick?" she said, half scolding, half laughing.

"Certainly not. I have been known to discuss the Corn Bill for a whole weekend without falling asleep—except in bed at night—and once discussed the nature of the Trinity with a bishop at Longleat for hours on end. At least I think it was the Trinity we were discussing. Or perhaps it was the Marquess of Bath and his son, the viscount. The father, son, and the ghost of Longleat—the famous Green Lady. I suit my conversation to the company. That will teach you to denigrate my nose."

Swann looked from one to the other in confusion. "Get a grip on yourself, Fen. You're bosky. The Green Lady of Longleat ain't a holy ghost. She ain't a nun. In fact, she was nothing else but a trollop, carrying on behind her husband's back."

"I stand corrected," Fen said.

"The reason I came," Swann continued, "the tea tray has been brought in. Some dandy-looking plum cake there, if you would like to get away from Fenwick's ridiculous stories and give it a try, Miss Lonsdale."

"An offer too good to refuse. From the ridiculous to the sublime—plum cake," Fenwick said, and offered Jane his arm.

Scawen took her other elbow and she was led back to the saloon in high style. There was no more bantering between her and Fenwick. They took their tea and plum cake in near silence, but something had changed between them. Fenwick looked at her in a different way, with quiet, intimate smiles, the way a gentleman looks at a lady he admires. It proved so disconcerting that Jane accidentally sugared her tea, when she had learned to like it with only milk at Miss Prism's.

After the gentlemen left, she could hardly believe she had spoken so freely with Lord Fenwick in the library. What had come over her, to say such things to a lord? What had come over him? Their conversation bordered on the flirtatious. At times it crossed the border. And she had enjoyed every moment of it. Was this how ladies with a fortune lived? It was lovely.

But it was only an amusement. Lord Fenwick might flirt with her when his own friends were not about, but he would never offer for a dowerless lady, even if she might inherit something from her aunt. She was just a pig in a poke, and Fenwick would look for a blue-blooded heiress.

Chapter Nine

"So she is coming," Lady Sykes said the next morning over breakfast. "And not even a written reply, when I made a point of writing 'RSVP' on the bottom of the cards. Just what one would expect of a housekeeper, but I own I am surprised a schoolmistress from Miss Prism's Academy does not know the proper way to reply to an invitation. I have had a written answer from Mr. Parker, you see," she said, holding up a note.

Swann frowned at this. "Why did you invite Parker?" he asked. Parker was a schoolteacher, and therefore a potential competitor for Miss Lonsdale's hand.

"I needed another gentleman to round out the table. I invited Mrs. Rogers, from Bibury. She has had me to tea twice. One must repay social obligations, Scawen."

"She has not had *me* to tea!"

Lady Sykes always repaid her social obligations on the backs of her friends when she could.

Scawen began counting up numbers on his fingers. "You are out in your reckoning," he said. "We have four ladies without Mrs. Rogers."

Lady Sykes was very seldom out in her ciphering. She knew numbers as a sawbones knew a body, from the inside out. "Nonsense. The house-keeper, the schoolmistress, and myself. That is three."

"You're forgetting Mama. She plans to attend."

Lady Sykes looked at him as if he had announced he was inviting the rat catcher. "On a litter, I assume? I trust that is your idea of a joke, Scawen. Your mama has not left her bed in a decade."

"Yes, she has. She often hobbles along to the end of the hall to look out at the swans. Anyhow, I told her you are having a party, and she says she must attend." A look of unusual severity seized his features, and he added, "Only fitting, as she is the hostess. It's her house."

"Nothing of the sort. It's your house, and it is your duty to see she doesn't come shambling in to spoil my party. I won't have it. She is eighty-five years old. She drools."

"Only eighty. Mama is a little vain about her age. She lies. She wants to come down to meet the ladies."

Scawen was a rock in the matter. He loved his mama. She had been in her forties when he was born, and as a consequence, he had been raised as if he were her grandson, with very lenient and loving care. Mrs. Swann would attend the party. She not only planned to attend, she had Swann and Fenwick carry her downstairs that morning to oversee the dinner preparations.

She sat in a Bath chair, a wizened little crone in a gown from the last century, missing half her teeth and half her hair. What hair remained was pretty, as white as the driven snow and inclined to curl, but the wisps were not enough to hide her

91

shiny pink scalp. She had dispensed with caps some twenty-odd years before. Caps made her head itchy. Her voice was weak, but it was not querulous. It laid down the law in a breathless, childish tone that brooked no interference.

"I want no promiscuous seating, Scawen," she said. Her lack of teeth caused a slurring of her speech that was not quite a lisp, but it tended in that direction. She did not deign to discuss her party with Phoebe.

"What the devil is she talking about?" Phoebe demanded. "There will be no promiscuity. It is a dinner party we are having, not an orgy."

"Gents on one side of the table; ladies on t'other. That is how it was done in my day," the little lady declared.

"Is she trying to make a fool of me?" Phoebe asked.

"Ladies proceed to the table first," Mrs. Swann continued, ignoring Phoebe. "Highest-ranking lady leads. That will be Lady Pargeter. I, as hostess, go last, followed by the gents. And I get to carve." Her trembling little hands gave a foretaste of the shambles she would make of carving.

Phoebe decided to try guile. "Oh, my dear Lavinia!" she laughed. "Your dainty little hands couldn't handle a carving knife. It would be too dangerous."

"In my day, ladies went to carving school. I came top of the class. I remember perfectly how to unbrace a mallard and unlace a coney, to rear a goose and allay a pheasant. I hope we are having pheasant, Scawen. We will want two courses, and I think four meat dishes and side dishes will suffice for a simple dinner party. And of course, a savory."

"Just as you wish," Mama," Scawen said.

Mrs. Swann's rheumy eyes turned to Fenwick. "Who is this young Adonis?" she demanded. "And why have you not been up to pay your respects to your hostess, eh?"

"I visited you the morning after I arrived, Mrs. Swann," he said. "Do you not recall, you told me I was a brass-faced monkey?"

"Ah, so that was you. Of course I remember. You brought me marchpane. It pulled out a molar, but it was loose anyhow, and it was worth it. Do you have any more marchpane for me?"

"I shall buy some the next time I am in Bibury."

"Why don't you go now? You have plenty of time. My party is not until this evening." She turned to Scawen. "Who is coming, Scawen? Who am I having this party for? Is it the Pargeters? Why am I entertaining them? They never have me to dinner. I haven't seen Wildercliffe in a decade, except for the chimney pots."

"We are inviting Miss Lonsdale and Lady Pargeter, Mama. You remember Miss Rampling?"

"Of course I remember Rampling. Is she coming? She used to call with Lizzie. No one calls on me nowadays. Push me toward the window, Scawen. I want to see the road. I cannot see the road from my window, just the chimney pots and the lake and those demmed swans."

Phoebe threw up her hands and went below stairs to speak to Cook, to see that the meat was carved when it arrived at the table. With luck, Lavinia would tire herself out before dinner, and be in her bed when the guests arrived.

At Wildercliffe that morning, Jane was also making plans for the dinner party. She examined her gowns, wishing she had one that was more stylish. Miss Prism did not permit the empress style that was all the crack in London. "Decadent!" she said, condemning them with a word. With great trepidation, Jane took the scissors to her evening gown and scooped out the neckline. Fay supplied her with Belgian lace to finish off the border. Sewing was a necessary skill for a vicar's daughter, and the job was done well. It did not look in the least homemade, but quite stylish. She would wear her one piece of good jewelry, the small string of pearls Papa had given Mama for a wedding gift.

Next she went to work on her hair. She customarily wore it bundled back in a bun, but it was naturally curly. She brushed it out at her mirror and tried arranging it in various styles. She and her friend Harriet often used to arrange each other's hair in their bedroom at night, to pass the time. But without Harriet to help her, the job proved difficult. The best she could do was to loosen the front curls somewhat, and pin the rest up in a roll across the back of her head. It looked rather elegant. Fay lent her a small diamond pin to set amidst the curls at the front. Before going below stairs for lunch, Jane resumed her usual coiffure.

By early afternoon, she sat at the desk in the Blue Saloon, writing a letter to Harriet Stowe. Her gaze often turned to the window toward Swann Hall, as she wondered if she would see Fenwick and Swann riding forth to visit her and Fay. They did not come, but at about three o'clock, Lord Fenwick called. He came not through the meadows but by the road, driving a spanking yellow curricle whose silver appointments twinkled in the sunlight. The rig was drawn by a pair of blood grays.

"I am just off to Bibury to buy Mrs. Swann some marchpane, and thought you might like to come with me," he said to Jane, after a few words of greeting to the ladies.

Jane's heart beat faster. She had never been in a curricle. She and Harriet used to watch them fly by, driven by the out and outers in Bath, and wish they might have a drive in such a dashing rig. And with Lord Fenwick by her side! She positively ached with pleasure, yet her voice, when she spoke, was calm.

"You don't mind if I go, Aunt Fay?"

"Run along, dear. There's little enough to amuse a youngster here. I shall have a rest."

"You really ought to have a walk about the park," Jane said.

"We'll do that after you return."

"I mean to hold you to that!" Jane said, in a scolding way. Then she ran for her bonnet and pelisse.

The drive was everything she had imagined, and more. Fenwick drove at a fast pace to impress her, when she admitted she had never been in a curricle before. She clung for dear life to the edge of the precarious perch, and could not restrain a little squeal of fearful delight when he took the corners at what seemed to her a reckless speed. Stone houses and fields of sheep spun past in a blur. Conversation was virtually impossible with the wind whistling in her ears, and so many new sensations to be enjoyed.

When they drove into town, heads turned to ogle them. Jane felt she was living in a dream. For this one brief hour, she was the pampered lady in the curricle with the dashing gentleman by her side, and not the poor creature gazing enviously as the rig whizzed past. She would include an account of the outing in her letter to Harriet.

"I look a quiz!" she exclaimed, clutching at her bonnet, when at last Fenwick drove into the inn yard to stable his rig.

He reached out, tucked a wanton curl back in place, straightened her bonnet, and said, "There, now you look like your proper little self."

The speech was at odds with the intimate gesture. Was that how he saw her, as a "proper little" lady? She felt she had grown beyond that. But then, what should he think, when she was wearing the horrid old round bonnet that Miss Prism insisted on? He hopped down and threw the reins to a stableboy, then assisted Jane down from the perch. He didn't offer his hand; such mild gestures were for old men, in Fenwick's view. He put his two hands around her waist and whirled her to the ground in a flurry of skirts that showed her ankles. His sharp eye noticed the lack of any lace on her petticoat. It also noticed her slender, well-turned ankles. His strong hands held her as easily as if she were a flower. She gave a little gasp of surprise, then laughed to cover her embarrassment.

"You should smile more often, Miss Lonsdale," he said, gazing at her upturned face. Lovely long lashes, she had, and such a delicate complexion. "You don't have to frighten your pupils now." He felt a stabbing ache for that plain muslin petticoat. A lady deserved lace.

"Oh, I never frighten them. Miss Prism is in charge of scaring the poor things to death."

"A shrew, is she? Did she frighten you, too?"

"Well, she is rather a Tartar, but let's not spoil this wonderful outing by talking about her."

Chapter Ten

"Which way shall we go?" Jane asked, looking
around. On an impulse she said, "I should like to
buy a new bonnet while we're here." Then she
added artlessly, "My aunt is paying me a shocking
salary for doing nothing but enjoying myself." He
looked a question at her. "Two hundred pounds per
annum," she announced, her eyes large with pleasure, verging on disbelief at her good fortune. "I
feel a very bandit taking it from her."

Fenwick felt a pang at the modest sum mentioned. He spent more than that on his boots. And
she spoke of this simple jaunt as "a wonderful outing." Lord, he was fortunate. Never had to work a
day in his life, and had more money than one man
could wisely spend. Free to come and go as he
wished, while other, no doubt more worthy, folks
toiled their lives away under the thumb of petty ty-
rants such as Miss Prism.

"I love helping ladies choose their bonnets," he
said. "I, being nothing else but a fashionable frib-
ble, shall advise you on all the latest London
modes, and you shall help me choose some marchpane for Mrs. Swann."

"I recommend the one with nuts and cherries. It's

lovely! Harriet—she's my friend at Bath—bought me some for my birthday."

"It won't do for Mrs. Swann. She has difficulty in chewing," he said discreetly, for it seemed rude to say she was missing half her teeth.

"Then you already know what you must buy. You don't need my help."

"I didn't invite you to come with me because I need help, Miss Lonsdale, but because I enjoy your company," he said, and tucking her hand under his arm, they set off down the High Street.

They stopped at the first milliner's shop they came to and looked in the window.

"That one is rather pretty," Jane said, admiring a navy glazed straw bonnet with a low poke.

Fenwick shook his head. "You're out of the classroom now, ma'am. Let us go for something a little more dashing. This is a shop for older ladies. Why, it doesn't even have a French name," he said, pointing to the sign that read *Miss Daly, Purveyor of Millinery to the Quality*. "All the better milliners pretend they're French, you must know."

"Yes, and charge twice the price for the honor of being able to say the bonnet came from Mademoiselle Dubois, instead of Miss Wood."

"But one is also allowed to call the bonnet a *chapeau*. That is worth something. A bonnet is like perfume. One pays for more than the actual product. It should make you feel feminine and alluring. What price can be put on that?"

"About a guinea, I should think. Bonnets are double the price in those pseudo-French shops. I like value for my hard-earned money."

"Actually, that was a rhetorical question. I see I

must watch my words with you. You are literal minded. I meant that no price is too high to pay for the satisfaction of knowing you look your best, being in style. You have two hundred pounds in your hot little hands. Don't be such a skint." When he saw her staring at him, he stopped. "God, I sound a fool!"

"You are the one who said it," she chided.

Jane didn't think he sounded foolish; only rich, and spoiled. Perhaps she would splurge and try a more stylish shop. They strolled along, stopping at various windows to look at the goods. Fenwick bought an enameled snuffbox from France, decorated with a copy of a Fragonard scene of a lady in a swing, because she reminded him of Jane. Its cost equaled a week of Jane's wages at the academy.

"I've never seen you use snuff," she mentioned.

"I don't," he admitted sheepishly, "but I happen to adore Fragonard. And it will make a handy container for headache powders or some such thing." He had a weakness for snuffboxes. A dozen of them sat on his toilet table at home, empty.

They stopped at the confectioner's, where Fenwick bought a box of plain marchpane for Mrs. Swann. While Jane chose some sweets as a present for Fay, he also bought a box of cherry and nut sweets for Jane, and had them both put in one parcel to keep hers as a surprise when they parted.

"Shall we get your bonnet next, or shall we pay our duty visit to the church first? Let us visit the church. Duty before pleasure, and I shall be carrying a hatbox once you have made your purchase. That is not a complaint, by the by."

"We don't *have* to visit the church," she said.

"Very well, let us save that treat for another outing and go to see the river instead."

The River Colne was hardly more than a stream, but it was pretty, with a couple of picturesque stone bridges spanning it. Across the bridge, the Arlington Row almshouses and the mill, built of stone like most of the local buildings, were the main features. The young couple strolled along in the sunshine, with a light breeze fanning their cheeks. As they returned, they stopped midway across the bridge to look at the water.

"Oh, look! There are fish!" Jane exclaimed, as the silver bodies flashed in the stream.

"Trout. By Jove, I wish I had my fishing rod. We would have fresh trout for dinner. But then that would spoil Mrs. Swann's menu," he added with a teasing laugh. "You are in for a rare evening, Miss Lonsdale."

"What do you mean?"

"I shan't spoil it by telling you, but I have a feeling Miss Prism would approve of how things are done *chez* Swann."

"How provoking you are! Do tell me."

"No, no. It's to be a surprise."

Jane gave a sigh. "If Miss Prism would approve, then I daresay we are having minced mutton and bread pudding."

Again Fenwick felt the familiar stab of pity. "Good Lord! Is that what she fed you?"

"Yes, and she charges such shocking prices. Imagine, feeding the daughters of gentlemen such wretched food."

"Imagine feeding Miss Lonsdale such a diet," he said, squeezing her fingers consolingly. "At least the gentlemen's daughters can eat properly when they go home."

"I, too, am a gentleman's daughter," she said with a rebukeful look.

He said hastily, "I was not implying otherwise. The *other* gentlemen's daughters, I should have said. I meant the students." He wondered at her leaping on his little slip, until it occurred to him how tenuous her hold on gentility had been, when she was left alone in the world. She guarded it fiercely, for without it she would be sunk beneath social redemption, reduced to some menial labor.

She accepted his explanation and said, "I shall never eat bread pudding again, as long as I live. I don't care if I starve, I shall never eat bread pudding again."

"You will not be offered it tonight, at any rate. It was not the food I meant, but—" She looked at him expectantly. "Never mind batting your long lashes at me, minx. I'm not going to spoil the surprise. Now, let us go and choose your bonnet."

They went to the other millinery shop in the village. Jane held that "long lashes" to her heart as though it were golden.

"Miss White's," he said, peering in the window. "Bibury is a decade behind the times. This should be Mademoiselle Blanche, for I see the *chapeaux* are a cut above Miss Daly's wares."

The prices were higher than Jane was accustomed to paying, but they were not exorbitant. She quelled down the urge to try on the more dashing bonnets Fenwick suggested, and chose a bonnet with a medium poke and a small rim, which just suited her modest style of beauty.

"It is you," Fenwick conceded, with more resignation than pleasure, as his eyes flickered over her plain serge pelisse.

"In other words, you think it's dowdy," she said.

"Don't put words in my mouth! I think it is eminently sensible, yet with a touch of distinction. Not a bonnet to turn heads, but a close examination shows its quality."

"I expect you mean well, but I would have preferred a flattering lie," she said, with that artless candor that he found amusing. "I'm tired of being sensible."

"Always happy to oblige, ma'am. That is the most ravishing bonnet it has ever been my privilege to set eyes on. It puts London bonnets to the blush."

"Thank you for the effort, but a compliment is no good when you have to *pry* it out of a gentleman."

"It really looks very nice," he said uncertainly.

She gave a *tsk* of disbelief, although he did think it looked nice. "Let us go back now," she said, when Miss White handed Fenwick the hatbox. "I want to make sure Aunt Fay takes some exercise. She's too idle, and she eats more than she ought, out of boredom. She'll fall into flesh if I let her."

Fenwick just shook his head. "Still a schoolteacher at heart, eh, Miss Lonsdale? You can take the teacher out of the schoolroom, but you cannot take the schoolroom out of the teacher."

"Since you have discovered my tendency to didacticism, then I might as well be killed for a sheep as a lamb. I think it was rash of you to buy a snuffbox when you don't take snuff."

Fenwick delved into his bag and handed her the

box of marchpane. "Here is salt for the wound, shrew! I not only squandered a whole guinea on a snuffbox, I also bought you this—and it isn't even your birthday. Go ahead, tell me it will ruin your teeth, or your complexion, or your figure. It's clear I can do nothing right."

Jane stared at the box, while a soft smile stole across her lips, and rose to lighten her eyes. She felt the most lowering fear she was going to cry. No gentleman had ever bought her bonbons before. She had to pinch her lower lip between her teeth to stop it from trembling.

"Thank you, Lord Fenwick," she said in a choked voice. "I hope I am not so ungracious as to say any of those things. That was very thoughtful of you." She peered into the box. "And it has cherries and nuts, too! You remembered."

"You're welcome," he said, embarrassed at her lavish praise.

"The snuffbox is very pretty," she said, with an air of apology.

A reluctant smile tugged at his lips. "You don't have to patronize me. My feelings are not so delicate as that."

"Is that what I was doing? I was trying to apologize for putting my oar in where it didn't belong."

"You were right. When you don't have to work for your money, you don't watch how you spend it. You're good for me, Aunt Jane. You will be reforming me if we aren't careful."

With a brash but charming smile, he took her elbow and accompanied her out of the shop. "Aunt Jane." She would not put that in her letter to Harriet. It cast a shadow on the afternoon's pleasure. So that was how he saw her, as a maiden aunt. And here she had thought he rather liked her.

Chapter Eleven

By the time Jane returned to Wildercliffe, it was too late to go out for a walk. Her aunt Fay had ventured into the garden at least. Jane found her taking the sun on the west terrace, which gave a view of the gardens, with rich fields behind, and in the distance the hazy green of trees. Strange to think all this vast estate belonged to her aunt. Almost impossible to believe that a working lady could end up a countess.

"I'm sorry we were so long," Jane said. "We went for a little walk. Lord Fenwick helped me pick out a new bonnet."

Her aunt looked at her askance. A glance showed her that Jane still wore the glow of pleasurable excitement. Fay was sorry to have to do it, but she felt she must disillusion the girl.

"I can see why any lady would be attracted to Fenwick, of course. He has that air of glamour. . . . But it would be foolish of you to expect anything to come of it, Jane. I don't want to see you hurt. Swann is your man, if you're on the lookout for a husband."

"I'm in no hurry, now that you and I are settled so comfortably here," she replied.

But her blush told the story. The foolish chit was

becoming too fond of Fenwick. "Nor am I in a hurry to lose you. Swann will be here long after Fenwick runs back to his London friends. We shall see if anything comes of it. Swann is a nice, comfortable fellow. If he had a wife to see he brushed his jacket and combed his hair, he would not be bad looking either."

Jane squeezed her aunt's hand. "Don't worry, Aunt Fay. I realize Fenwick is above my touch. Just let me enjoy these few days of such high company. I felt like a princess, walking on his arm in Bibury."

"Just so you realize you won't be walking down the aisle with him."

They soon went in to begin their toilettes. Lady Pargeter, determined to provoke Lady Sykes, wore her richest gown of black velvet, and the showy Pargeter diamond necklace that was much too grand for the occasion, but when would she have another chance to flaunt it in Phoebe's face?

Although Jane looked less impressive, she did not resemble a schoolteacher, or anyone's maiden aunt. The new hairdo lent her a touch of town bronze. Excitement put a sparkle in her eyes, and a glow on her cheeks. Her aunt Fay took one look at Jane's aging pelisse and sent off for a cashmere shawl.

Much to Lady Sykes's chagrin, Mrs. Swann was not only wide-awake for the dinner party, but so eager for it that she had her Bath chair pushed into the hallway to greet the guests.

"Ah, Rampling!" she exclaimed in a wavering voice, when the ladies were shown in. "I did not know I had invited you. But where are the Pargeters? Did you not come with them?"

Lady Pargeter ignored the question and gave the old lady a peck on the cheek. "It's wonderful to see you again, Mrs. Swann. How well you are looking."

Mrs. Swann wore a yellow brocade gown that had not been the height of fashion thirty years before, when she had had it made up. The lace had gone beyond yellow; it was snuff brown. She had shriveled to such an extent that the dress hung loosely from her gaunt shoulders. From the waist down she was wrapped in a blanket, to ward off the chill from the front door.

"I am doing pretty well for a lady who is pushing a hundred," she said with wild exaggeration. "But where are the Pargeters?"

Swann heard the commotion and came into the hallway. Phoebe was not far behind him. "This is Lady Pargeter, Mama," Swann said.

"Rubbish! I know Rampling to see her. Do you think I am loony?"

"Lady Pargeter, welcome to Swann Hall," Phoebe said, and gave Fay's hand a brief shake. Her sharp eyes took in the velvet gown, the sparkle of diamonds. She turned to Jane to conceal her annoyance. "And Miss Lonsdale. My, you do look nice," she said, running her eyes over the chit. She saw Miss Lonsdale had made an effort to update her appearance. "Just right for a small party. So vulgar to overdress. It is the mark of the parvenue."

"Who is this girl?" Mrs. Swann demanded, staring rudely at Jane. "Don't tell me you've finally nabbed a girl, Scawen! Good for you. She's not nearly so bad as I feared you would end up with. But where are the Pargeters?"

Lady Pargeter took the easiest way of pacifying the old malkin. "Unfortunately, the Pargeters couldn't come, Mrs. Swann. They send their regrets."

"Damme! Not coming, after I have laid on a veritable feast. I shan't ask them again, rude bints. Well, as you are here, you might as well come into the saloon."

Scawen took the ladies' wraps while Morton wheeled her chair into the saloon. Jane hardly glanced at Horace Gurney, nursing a glass of wine in the corner. Her first interest upon joining the party was to determine that Lord Fenwick was there, as indeed he was—looking quite devastatingly handsome in a deep mulberry jacket with a ruby in his cravat. He rose upon the ladies' entrance and made his bows. He was too suave to embarrass Jane by complimenting her in front of the group, but he lifted his eyebrows and gave an approving nod to acknowledge her new coiffure and more stylish gown.

As he showed her to a chair, he said quietly, "Well, well, Mademoiselle Lonsdale. Why have you been hiding your light under a round bonnet? I like that coiffure. It suits you admirably."

She said, "Thank you," and immediately rushed on to speak of Mrs. Swann.

Fenwick was not ready to discontinue his compliments and flirting that quickly. "You were supposed to inquire why I called you mademoiselle, literalist! That would have given me an opening to compliment you on your gown. I wager you did not wear that *chez* Prism." His eyes just flickered over the expanse of creamy bosom, with a demure ruffle of lace suggesting more than it revealed.

"I did, actually. I changed the neckline this morning."

"Most felicitously."

"Fay gave me the lace. It's real Belgian."

Mrs. Swann had been speaking in a loudish voice all the while. She proved impossible to ignore.

"I see Lizzie lent you her diamonds, Rampling. And a fancy gown as well, but that don't make up for her not coming, damned if it does. All my work. Pheasants, a dandy spring lamb, a turbot—to say nothing of the asparagus—and now the Pargeters are not coming, if you please. And never a note to warn me. I call that shabby."

Lady Sykes smiled a foxy smile and said, "It was very ill bred of Lady Pargeter not to reply to a written invitation. I must agree with you there, Mrs. Swann." She did not look within a right angle of the housekeeper, but she knew her arrow would reach its mark.

Mrs. Swann's rheumy eyes toured the room and settled on Jane. "So you are Scawen's lady," she announced. "Come here and let me get a good look at you."

Scawen turned beet red and said, "This is Lady Pargeter's niece, Mama."

"Rubbish! Lizzie has no niece."

"She is my niece," Fay said.

"Your niece, Rampling? Does she have any dot? Scawen has to marry at least a small fortune. Swann Hall is falling apart."

"Miss Lonsdale was a schoolmistress," Lady Sykes explained.

"No money at all, then? Dear me, what a pity, for she would make an excellent wife. A nice plump bosom on her, and a good wide hip. She would give you a nurseryful ere long, Scawen. Has she any prospects at all? A rich uncle?"

Fenwick's eyes slid to Jane, expecting to see her writhing in embarrassment. She sat, nice as a nun, smiling at Mrs. Swann.

"Miss Lonsdale has a wealthy aunt," Fay said.

Mrs. Swann hit her knee and crowed, "Excellent! You want to keep on terms with the lady, Miss Lonsdale. There is nothing like money when all is said and done. A pretty face soon falls into ruin, but gold keeps its sheen." She then turned her troublesome attentions to her son. "Snap her up while you can, Scawen. You cannot expect to do better, for there is no denying you have no looks at all, and very little conversation, though you was always good-hearted."

"Heh heh," Swann said. "I would not say no if Miss Lonsdale asked me."

"Gudgeon!" his mama scolded. "Is that how the world wags nowadays, the ladies offering for the gentlemen? I knew Prinney was destroying society with his carrying on, but I did not realize it had come to this. Am I having any more guests, Scawen?"

"Mrs. Rogers and Mr. Parker are coming, Mama. He is a schoolteacher."

"Surely not from the parish school!"

"No, a very select private school for young gentlemen."

"He is a gentleman," Lady Sykes inserted. "He wrote a card accepting."

"I shall not brave the draft from the front door for a schoolteacher," Mrs. Swann said. She pulled at her blankets and said querulously, "What is keeping him? I want my dinner."

She was pacified with a glass of wine, and before long Mr. Parker was shown in, accompanied by

Mrs. Rogers, the widow of the late vicar of the parish. She was a jolly lady of middle years, wearing a puce gown. Her fulsome figure provided a comical contrast to Mr. Parker's cadaverous frame. He was a tall, thin gentleman in an ill-fitting jacket whose cuffs were bereft of nap. Everything about him looked undernourished. His long face was emaciated and the unappetizing color of a slug. Even his hair was thin and colorless, not quite gray, yet not blond or brown either. It hung lank about his unprepossessing face.

"Good day, Mrs. Rogers," Mrs. Swann said. Mrs. Rogers came to shake her hand before taking a seat. Mrs. Swann then turned her attention to Parker. "He is a long drink of water," she informed the company.

Lady Sykes introduced the new arrivals, taking care to end up with Parker at Jane's chair. "Miss Lonsdale is also a schoolteacher," she said. "You two will have plenty to talk about. Do you mind giving Mr. Parker your chair, Fenwick?"

She could not trust the way Fenwick was running after Miss Lonsdale. Of course, there was no danger of his offering for her, but he might give her ideas above her station. If he put the notion of having a Season into her head, for instance, Nigel would be hard-pressed to nab her, for she really looked very pretty this evening.

"Pray, do not disturb yourself, Lord Fenwick," Parker said, unaware of the burden resting on his narrow shoulders. He got himself a chair, which he drew up to Jane's other side.

"So you are a fellow teacher, Miss Lonsdale," he said, with the sympathetic eye of a fellow sufferer.

"I was teaching in Bath, but I have given it up. I'm my aunt's companion now, at Wildercliffe."

"Ah! A wonderful place, Wildercliffe."

"Yes, it's magnificent."

They spoke a little about Wildercliffe, then he told her about the school where he taught. When Jane felt she had done her duty, she turned back to Fenwick.

"You mentioned there was to be some unusual feature at this dinner party, Lord Fenwick. Was it Mrs. Swann's outspoken way you referred to, or are further treats in store?"

"The gaiety has hardly begun. I want to compliment you on your forbearance, ma'am. I daresay some ladies would blush to hear their physical charms trumpeted so loudly in public. You took it like a rock."

"She meant no harm. At her age, you know, she hardly realizes what she is saying."

"Yet she's not lacking in wit. She knows a prime catch when she sees one."

"Yes, and she knows the importance of a dowry, too."

"I want my mutton!" Mrs. Swann exclaimed in a loud voice, just as Morton came to announce dinner.

Chapter Twelve

Mrs. Swann clapped her hands. "Now we are in a pickle!" she said. "I counted on Lady Pargeter to lead the parade. The highest-born lady gets to go first. We will have no promiscuous seating at my table. Ladies go first."

Jane looked at Fenwick. "Promiscuous seating? What does she mean?"

"It's not the racy sort of thing the name suggests. One envisages sitting with a lady on his lap, peeling grapes and spilling wine, but it refers only to ladies and gentlemen sitting side by side. Even that lechery is forbidden us tonight. Ladies on one side of the table, gents on the other, like a country dance."

Mrs. Swann's voice trumpeted out again. "You will lead us in, Lady Sykes, even if you ain't a real lady. Only a baronet's widow."

Lady Pargeter stood aside. "Age before beauty," she said in a low voice, but not so low that Lady Sykes could not hear it.

"I hardly know how to arrange the rest of you," Mrs. Swann said, regarding her motley crew of guests. "A schoolteacher, a companion, and a vicar's wife. I daresay you are second in consequence, Mrs. Rogers. Then Rampling and her niece, and I shall go at the end of the crocodile's tail. The gentlemen follow behind, also in order of consequence. Lord Fenwick, you may lead, followed by Gurney and Parker. I don't know exactly who Mr. Gurney is, or what he is doing here. You're no one, are you, Mr. Gurney? No one special, I mean." He shook his head, smiling. "Anyhow, the host brings up the rear. All in a line, now. And mind where you sit. Ladies on one side of the board, gents on t'other."

The guests, exchanging puzzled looks, did as the old lady ordered. "Parting is such sweet sorrow," Fenwick said, assisting Jane from her chair. "And I shan't even have the pleasure of sitting across the board from you."

"Certainly not. I shall be below the salt. Are we allowed to talk across the table?"

"Bite your tongue, Miss Lonsdale! I doubt if we are even allowed to look at the opposite sex. There may be a set of blinkers at our plate. I wish I had brought a good book to bear me company. Mrs. Radcliffe, for choice."

"Well, Miss Prism always told us that a lady does not complain. All experiences are broadening, so away we go."

He watched as she swept away, still smiling valiantly. The lady had countenance. Not a word of complaint. She actually found something useful in this farouche affair.

Other than the peculiar manner of seating, the dinner party was not radically different from any other dinner. Both the head and foot of the table were left vacant, so that those at the end of the board had only one partner. To put the host and hostess there would involve seating a gentleman beside a lady. Jane sat at the end, beside her aunt

Fay and across from Mr. Parker. Mrs. Swann was so busy gobbling her food that she did not object when the guests spoke across the table. Mr. Parker seldom went into company. He latched on to Jane like a drowning man, perhaps because his side companion was Horace Gurney, who preferred to converse with his wineglass.

"What subjects do you teach?" Parker asked her, and she told him English was her main subject, with some lessons in deportment. Of course, she reciprocated and asked him what he taught.

"Latin and Greek," he said proudly. "I studied the classics at Oxford, and prepare the older boys for university. Education is the *sine qua non* of a gentleman, do you not agree, Miss Lonsdale?"

"Oh indeed, and I would add the same applies to ladies, in a lesser degree, of course."

"Aere perennius." Seeing her blank look, he translated, "More lasting than brass—education endures forever."

"The classics are a useful ornament for gentlemen, I daresay, for sprinkling on speeches and things, but for every day, I have never felt the lack of Latin and Greek to be a drawback." Until now, she added to herself.

"I am willing *audire alteram partem*, as you might say."

The conversation continued, partly in English, partly in Latin and Greek, and mostly in confusion on Jane's side. It was almost a relief when Parker began to quiz her about her own work.

"Miss Prism's is an excellent school!" he said. "It turns out a well-finished young lady. My aunt used to work there. She is retired now."

"Is she married?" Jane asked.

"Oh no. It is an axiom that Miss Prism's ladies are married to their work. She still lives in Bath, and sees her old friend Miss Prism often. I shall tell her I met you."

Jane felt an awful churning inside, yet she could hardly ask him not to mention her. She hoped that, like many casual conversations, this one would be forgotten as soon as the evening was over. Course followed course, until even Mrs. Swann was sated. Phoebe's instructions to the cook obviated the necessity of the hostess's doing any carving, except on her own plate.

"Now it is time for us ladies to leave the gentlemen to their port," Mrs. Swann said, pushing her chair back as she could not rise from it. "Don't let the company overindulge, Scawen," she cautioned, as the footman wheeled her out. She glanced at Horace Gurney, whose eyes were closed, his head resting on his chest. "Especially that one," she added. "Wretched manners, to overindulge at the dinner table. I don't know what that fellow is doing here."

Lady Sykes was not tardy to escape to the saloon, where Mrs. Swann's ill nature was easily diverted to tearing Lady Pargeter apart for not coming to her party. Lady Sykes quite enjoyed herself, as the conversation allowed many slurs on the missing guest, each accompanied by a look that told Fay which Lady Pargeter she referred to, and it was not the late Lady Pargeter. Fay just patted her diamonds and smiled.

Ere long, the gentlemen joined them. Jane looked hopefully to Fenwick, but it was Mr. Parker who was legging it toward her, his eyes gleaming with the hope of impressing her with more Latin and

Greek. Mrs. Swann rescued her by commanding Mr. Parker to join her and tell her all about himself. Unfortunately, Lord Fenwick was caught in the toils of Mrs. Rogers, who had met a lady who knew his mama, and wanted to tell him all about it. Until the tea tray arrived, Scawen sat with Jane, apologizing and complimenting her.

"Mama meant no harm," he said. "It's just her little way. She likes you very much. Who would not?"

"I like her, too, Mr. Swann. I was not offended by her remarks, I promise you."

"That is demmed decent of you, considering what she said about your—er, well, your body actually."

"I believe she meant those comments as compliments."

"Oh, certainly. And I agree. That is to say—By Jove, here is the tea tray," he said, and darted off to recover his wits.

Mr. Parker also moved when the tea tray arrived. His pale eyes turned to Jane. Before he could grab a cup, Fenwick came forward and handed her one.

"I have brought you some tea to keep you awake," he said, sitting beside her. "I had to move quickly to outrun Parker's long legs, but I spare no pains when it comes to rescuing a damsel in distress. Well, Miss Lonsdale, how do you like the pentagon that is forming around you?"

"Please speak English, milord. I have had enough Latin for one evening."

"Pentagon comes from the Greek, actually. As a schoolteacher yourself, you will pardon my foray into didacticism. A pentagon is a five-sided figure, having nothing to do with female swans, so far as I know. Mr. Parker has knocked our neat square out of kilter with his attentions. Was it perfectly dreadful, Miss Lonsdale? You are such a stoic, it's hard to tell whether you were only bored, or ready to pick up your knife and stab him."

"I was not so much bored as confused. I found myself wishing I knew German or Sanskrit, to show him how annoying it is to be spoken to in a foreign tongue. I prefer plain old Anglo-Saxon."

"Even when it involves bosoms and hips?" he asked, with a laughing look. "She really is the limit. I adore her. Where else would you find such an original? If she were fifty or sixty years younger, I would make her my new flirt. Buy myself a Bath chair and go on the strut—er, wheel—together on Bond Street. Ply her with marchpane until I had the last tooth out of her head."

"I do like her, in spite of all," Jane said. "It's so refreshing to meet someone who says exactly what she thinks." It occurred to her that this was also part of Fenwick's charm. Lady Swann was outspoken because she was senile; Fenwick, because he was so sure of himself, he didn't have to worry what anyone thought. Scawen had not used the words "bosoms" and "hips," but Fenwick did not hesitate to do so.

"I agree. There has been a deal of double entendre here this evening, with Phoebe and Fay sniping at each other. When I am angry or jealous, I prefer to just come out with it, so I shall say without demur that I do not care for your Mr. Parker. 'I would have men about me that are fat. Yon Parker has a lean and hungry look.' You may now inquire with feigned obtuseness whether I speak from anger or jealousy, Miss Lonsdale."

"I can't see that you have anything to be jealous of, so I must assume you are angry with him."

"Just so. It would be infra dig for a marquess to admit he was jealous of a schoolmaster, so I shall pretend I'm angry that he stole the place I wanted at the table. That is the trouble when one's pentagons have so many masculine angles."

"I didn't realize that angles have gender. What, pray, is a masculine angle?"

"Why, to be sure, men are the obtuse angles. The ladies, I have noticed, are usually acute."

Their flirtation was interrupted by the arrival of Scawen, balancing a teacup in one hand. He drew a chair up and sat down, sloshing tea into his saucer.

"Just giving the old ears a bit of a rest," he said. "Parker collared me at the tea table. Was asking me about some Pelopon war. Daresay it's Latin for the Peninsular War. What was you two talking about?"

"You, and three other gentlemen, and a lady," Fenwick replied.

"Eh? What was you saying about me? Three men and a lady. I never—heh heh." Fenwick glinted a nervous smile at Jane. "It was about Mama, I suppose. I already apologized to Miss Lonsdale. Mind you, the dinner was dandy, barring the seating."

"It was delightful, Mr. Swann," Jane said. "It is your turn to dine with us next. Aunt Fay will be in touch with you shortly."

"Look forward to it. And now I must get Mama to bed. I see she is nodding off. She's not usually up so late. The excitement has gone to her head. Or perhaps it was the wine."

Everyone gathered to take their leave of Mrs. Swann. "Come again soon," she said, smiling all around and waving her hand.

While they were on the move, Mrs. Rogers decided it was time to leave. Mr. Parker had come with her, and also took his leave, making a special foray in Jane's direction to say good night to her, in hope of being invited to call at Wildercliffe. Jane feared this would only encourage him to speak to his aunt, who was on visiting terms with Miss Prism, and withheld the invitation. Scawen encouraged the party from Wildercliffe to remain, but Lady Pargeter was looking fatigued, and Jane left with her.

"How did you like your future mama-in-law?" Fay asked, and laughed heartily. "What an evening. And on top of it all, I ate too much. I feel nauseous."

"Mr. Parker was a bore. He has an aunt who used to work for Miss Prism. I hope he doesn't call on me. I ignored his hints."

"I invited the folks from Swann Hall to dinner the day after tomorrow. I shall need the extra day to prepare. We won't invite Parker."

"I'm glad you're back on terms with one set of neighbors at least."

"Two sets. I shall invite Lord Malton as well. That will give Lady Sykes something to think about."

"I wish you two could get along better. She's very nice to me."

"You must not deprive us older ladies of our little animosities, Jane. They give spice to life. I don't really dislike Lady Sykes. Under different circumstances, we could be friends. To tell the truth, I pity her—and she envies me. I rose higher than she. It is only we who were not so highly born as the company we find ourselves in who rip and claw at each other. I shall miss her, when she goes."

It was sad to think of Swann Hall without its guests. Jane knew she would miss Fenwick, too.

Chapter Thirteen

Lady Pargeter was ill during the night. Jane heard her in distress and went to her assistance.

"I think it's food poisoning," Fay gasped.

"Shall I send for the doctor?" Jane asked.

But when Fay had cast up her accounts, she felt better and decided against sending for Dr. Cassidy. Jane sat with her until she was sure her aunt was not going to have a relapse.

"I wonder if Lady Sykes slipped something into my food," Fay said. She looked wan and weak as she lay back against the pillows, lit only by the flicker of a lamp.

"Surely you're joking!"

"She thinks Nigel will inherit Wildercliffe if I die. But no, I do not think she would go this far. Seafood often disagrees with me. No doubt that is the culprit. I'm feeling better now. Go back to bed, Jane."

Jane said, "I shall just sit with you until you doze off." She poured a glass of wine to while away the early morning vigil. When her aunt was sleeping peacefully, Jane returned to her own room.

She slept in the next morning. Fay was at the table, looking a little hagged after her troubled night but by no means ill, when Jane came downstairs.

In fact, Fay had a full plate of gammon and eggs sitting in front of her. After eating only a little, she said, "Oh dear. I feel the nausea coming on again!" and fled from the table.

She was soon back. She was not sick to her stomach on that occasion, but Jane was concerned about her. "Let me call the doctor," she said, two or three times, until Fay agreed.

Fay retired to her bedchamber, and Jane brooded over a cup of coffee until Dr. Cassidy arrived. Jane accompanied him to her aunt's bedchamber, but was dismissed while he made his examination.

Jane rushed out to meet him when he came downstairs. "Is my aunt all right?" she asked.

"She is fit as a fiddle," he said. "She should get plenty of rest, take daily exercise outdoors, weather permitting, and limit her drinking of wine."

"I shall see that your orders are followed," Jane said, happy to have her own ideas of a healthy regimen confirmed by an expert.

"At her age, one cannot be too cautious. But she's fine. I foresee no difficulty."

"She's not that old," Jane said, surprised.

He gave a frowning pause. "She's not so young as she might be. Well, I am off to see Mr. Willis. He nearly severed a finger in a sawing accident yesterday. Good day, Miss Lonsdale. I shall look in on your aunt from time to time. Be sure to call me if there is any trouble."

She thanked him, and accompanied him to the doorway.

Lady Pargeter was up and about by lunchtime, with no apparent ill effects from her bout of nausea. It was the day Jane was to go to Bibury with Mr. Swann, but she felt she ought not to leave her aunt alone. When she mentioned this to Fay, her aunt overrode her.

"Run along, Jane. I'm delighted to see you and Swann hitting it off. I have plenty to occupy me, arranging my dinner party. I shall put it off a few days. It seems almost impolite to return the invitation so soon, as if one did not want to be in arrears. Having them back so soon gives it the air of a duty, rather than a pleasure. I plan to enjoy my little dinner party. Lord Malton promised to drop in this afternoon, so I shan't be alone. I'll ask him to accompany me on a walk about the park, as Cassidy recommended. It will do Malton good as well."

When Mr. Swann arrived, he had Fenwick with him. Swann was so unaccustomed to courting that it never occurred to him he was ruining his chances by bringing along a gentleman ten times more attractive than himself. He had some vague notion in his head that the outing would be livelier with Fenwick along. Miss Lonsdale would like it.

And indeed Miss Lonsdale was delighted to see this enlargement of the outing. For all his good qualities, there was no getting around the fact that Swann was unattractive. His wrinkled jacket, on this occasion, was decorated with bits of fluff that turned out to be swansdown. He had spent his morning at the lake with his gun, keeping an eye on his cygnets. He had spotted a falcon nearby, and didn't want to lose one of his precious brood.

The three set out for Bibury in Swann's lumbering carriage. It was ancient, the side walls wearing a season's coat of dust. The team drawing it was an indifferent set of bay plodders. The left rear wheel squeaked for lack of oil. Swann, however, noticed nothing amiss.

"A dashed fine day," he said, smiling amiably. "I thought you might like to have a look at the church, Miss Lonsdale. Or have you visited it already?"

"I haven't been in it. I should like to see it."

"A dashed fine church. Norman. That's French."

"Yes."

"There's a river in town as well. It has no swans. You might see a clutch of ducks, I daresay. Really a very nice little town, Bibury."

"Yes. Picturesque," she replied.

Seeing that the outing was not rolling along in such a jolly manner as it might, Swann cast an appealing eye on Fenwick.

Fenwick interpreted the look and tried to oblige. "This talk of churches and rivers is all very well, Scawen, but you must know that when a lady visits a village, what she is really interested in is the shops."

"Oh, we have shops," Swann assured Jane.

"We're not speaking of butcher shops and greengrocers," Fenwick rattled on. "What an out and outer like Miss Lonsdale wants to see is the drapery shop, and the ladies' toy stores."

"I make no claim to being an out and outer," Jane objected.

"Such modesty, and you wearing the most ravishing bonnet ever devised!" Fenwick said, glancing at her new low poke in a deliciously conspiratorial way. "Of course, you're a dasher, but it doesn't do for a lady to do her own crowing. That is our duty, eh, Swann?"

"Yes, by Jove. A regular out and outer. You will show all the gels the way, Miss Lonsdale."

"No doubt that Norman church will be full of low

poke bonnets in emulation of your new *chapeau*, come Sunday," Fenwick said.

The ride and especially the conversation continued at a merry pace until they reached Bibury, where they stabled the carriage and went on the strut. It was a rare treat for Jane to be walking out with not one, but two gentlemen. She gained her fair share of ogles, but it was at Fenwick that the ladies took a second look.

"Let us get the church over with first," Swann said, and set out at an ambling gait for the far end of the High Street. "There it is," he said, when it came into view.

It was a squat stone church built in the Norman style with rounded window and door. Swann just pointed to it. He had no details to add regarding its age, history, or construction.

"That's that," he said. "Or would you like to step inside and see the—the windows and pews and pulpit and all that, Miss Lonsdale?"

"I shall see them on Sunday. It's such a fine day, let us continue our walk."

They just glanced in at the various shops as they strolled toward the bridge, where they stopped to look for ducks. Swann formed a horn of his fingers around his lips and emitted a creditable imitation of a duck. When the birds paddled toward him, he pulled a handful of bread crusts out of his pocket. A shower of crumbs filled the air and clung to his coat and trousers as he broadcast the dry bread. Half a dozen birds came swimming forth to gobble up the crumbs.

"Now we have seen the church and river. What would you like to do next, Miss Lonsdale?"

As a stranger in the neighborhood, Jane had

nothing to suggest except to walk back to the shopping area.

"How about an ice?" Fenwick suggested.

"A nice what?" Swann asked, frowning. "Oh, you mean a nice cup of tea. Good idea, Fenwick. We shall just ankle along to Miss Daugherty's Tea Room."

"I believe Lord Fenwick meant an ice," Jane said, speaking slowly and clearly.

Swann considered it a moment. "He can have an ice at Miss Daugherty's if he wants. You and I shall have a nice cup of tea."

Jane would have preferred an ice, but she went along without complaint. The tea room was a modest affair with five tables, two of them against the windows, giving a view of the street beyond.

"We shall sit by the window where we can see the crowds passing by," Swann said, drawing a chair for Jane.

She glanced out the window, where one housewife hurried past, carrying a parcel, and two boys played with a dog.

"There is Bibury High Street," Swann said, pointing to the street they had just left as if it were an entirely new feature.

Jane feared Fenwick would say something that might offend Swann. "I thought it was Paree," he might say, or some such thing, but he just smiled at her, with a lambent glow in his eyes. "Does Miss Daugherty still make that gingerbread?" he asked Scawen.

"Yes, by Jove. The best gingerbread in the Cotswolds," Swann said. "I thought you was having an ice, Renshaw."

"I changed my mind. We cannot let the ladies have all the prerogatives."

"Eh? I am sure there will be plenty to go around. If there ain't, Miss Lonsdale can have my piece. I can have a gingerbread any time."

Miss Daugherty was able to provide sufficient tea and gingerbread for all three. Swann settled back with a sigh of contentment as Jane poured.

"I like to see a lady pour tea," he said. "It's homey, somehow. I picture long winter evenings by the grate, with Miss—with a lady pouring tea, and a hound curled up at my feet. You don't get that in London, Fenwick."

"Tea, hounds, and grates—and of course, ladies— are all available in London."

"Aye, but you don't know enough to stay at home and enjoy 'em. You're always gadding about to balls and routs and plays. You don't fool me," Swann said wisely.

"For shame, Fenwick," Jane said, then turned to Swann. "Milk and sugar?"

"Plenty of both." She fixed Swann's tea and handed it to him. "Here you go. A nice cup of tea."

"You pour very nicely, Miss Lonsdale, if you don't mind my saying so. Very dainty. You didn't spill a drop." He took the cup and promptly sloshed tea into his saucer.

"Thank you, Mr. Swann. I never balk at a compliment."

As he lifted the cup to his lips, drops of tea fell to his waistcoat, to join the feathers and dust and bread crumbs there. Jane had to restrain herself from chiding him, as she was accustomed to doing with her awkward students.

"Just milk for me," Fenwick said. They exchanged a look half of dismay, half of amusement, at Swann's performance.

As Swann lifted his cup, loosing another shower of drops, Jane could no longer restrain herself. "The tea is dripping on your waistcoat, Mr. Swann," she said. "Perhaps if you dried your saucer with the napkin . . ."

He looked down. "By Jove! So it is. What I need is a wife to smarten me up. Heh heh. Someone to tell me what to do." He daubed at the tea, while darting a shyly hopeful look at Jane. What he needed was a nanny, but she could hardly say so without hurting his feelings.

Jane wished Fenwick would begin some of his lively bantering, but he had fallen silent, with a small frown puckering his forehead. It was Scawen's rather awkward hint that he saw Miss Lonsdale in the role of his wife that accounted for it. He knew Scawen liked Jane, but until that moment, he hadn't realized Swann was serious about her. It would be an excellent thing for them both. Scawen certainly needed a wife, and Miss Lonsdale would be doing well for herself to nab him. She was a good-natured lady who didn't seem to mind his awkwardness and lack of conversation.

He was attracted to her himself; she was different from his usual sophisticated flirts, but he had no serious attachment. The decent thing to do was to retire from the fray. Scawen didn't meet many eligible ladies, whereas he knew a dozen girls who were as pretty as Jane, all of them with handsome dowries. It would be ill done of him to interfere in this romance. And so he sat, frowning into his cup, steeling himself to do the proper thing.

As soon as the tea was gone, he said, "Well, I

think that about does it for Bibury. Shall we be getting home?"

"If we hustle, we'll be just in time for tea," Swann said.

Jane stared at him, then she looked at Fenwick, expecting to see him chewing back a smile. He was fishing in his pocket for a coin to pay for the tea and gingerbread. She thought perhaps he had not heard that last bit of nonsense.

As they drove home, Fenwick mentioned that he must be continuing on to his hunting box soon. He spoke to Swann, but darted a look to Jane to see her reaction. She didn't object, but he noticed she drew her underlip between her teeth, as if disappointed.

"I wish you would stay a little longer," Swann said. He knew his outing with Miss Lonsdale required a third presence. "Just a day or two."

"Lady Pargeter is planning a dinner party in a few days," Jane said. "Why do you not wait until it is over, Lord Fenwick? We might have need of a peacemaker."

Fenwick felt there was still the possibility that Lady Alice Merton was on his trail. It might be best to remain a few days longer in hiding. He said, "I leave ladies' disputes severely alone."

"If you're talking about Phoebe and Rampling, I would hardly call it a severe dispute," Swann said. "More like a squabble. Ladies are always scratching at each other."

"I must take objection to that!" Jane said at once.

"No, but I was talking about ladies," Swann said.

Fenwick darted a smile at her. "Not that you ain't a lady, Miss Lonsdale."

"Exactly!" Swann agreed. "Other ladies. You are a nice quiet sort of girl."

"Thank you for the 'girl,' Mr. Swann. I am no longer in my teens."

"Well, an old girl. I am five and thirty myself. You seem like a girl to me." Then he turned to Renshaw. "Is it agreed you're staying a little longer, Fen?" he asked hopefully.

Fenwick saw the mute appeal in Scawen's eyes, and the hope in Jane's, and he wavered. "Perhaps a day or two," he said.

The gentlemen left Jane at the front door of Wildercliffe. Swann mentioned that he wouldn't call that evening as he had to attend a meeting of the Parish Council. Jane dallied a moment, hoping that Fenwick would invite himself to call, but he just drew a piece of paper out of his pocket and examined it. He took his leave politely, but she sensed some new reserve in him.

Lady Pargeter had just returned from her walk with Lord Malton and sat in the Blue Saloon, having tea, when Jane entered.

"Ah, your niece is back," Malton said, rising to bow to Jane. "I shall run along now, Fay. I am happy you've finally called in Cassidy. He will see no harm comes to you."

He left at once. "What did he mean, you have 'finally' called Cassidy?" Jane asked. "Have you had some problems before, Aunt Fay?"

"A touch of flu early in the spring. I was telling Lord Malton about it. He feels I am run-down. How did your visit go?"

"Fine. Lord Fenwick plans to leave soon. Will you have your dinner party before he goes?"

"I thought Friday evening might do. Lord Malton has agreed to come. Let us plan our menu."

They passed the interval until dinner in this agreeable fashion. Jane's mind was half-occupied with Fenwick, and the sudden change in his manner to her. It was only when she was changing for dinner that she remembered Lord Malton's remark about Fay finally calling Cassidy. Fay did not appear to be run-down. In fact, she was a little plumper than before, due to her sedentary way of going on, and her eating too many snacks. Being run-down would not cause nausea in any case. Was it possible Aunt Fay had some more serious illness? But illness usually caused a loss of weight.

For a long moment Jane stood, gazing into the mirror, but seeing an image of her aunt, with her increasing stomach. Of course! She was blind not to have seen it before! The nausea, the hunger, the fatigue. Aunt Fay was enceinte!

Chapter Fourteen

It was impossible to quiz Lady Pargeter over dinner, with the footmen hovering about, but as soon as the ladies retired to the saloon, Jane said quietly, "When is the baby due, Aunt Fay?"

Fay's sharp intake of breath was the only indication of surprise. It soon gave way to relief that the matter was out in the open.

"So you have twigged to it. Then it will not be long before the rest of the world knows it as well." She looked down at her increasing body.

"It can't be hidden much longer. What is the secret? You're married—or were at least. It's not as though the child were illegitimate."

"It's the timing," Fay said, and put her hand to her forehead. "It must have happened the first time we—you know what I mean. And you know what folks will say! That I trapped Pargeter into marriage. We were never—intimate until after the marriage, Jane. I hope you know me well enough to believe that."

"Of course I believe you! Good gracious, you don't have to explain yourself to me. I only asked when is the baby due."

"In six months. That will be nine months from the wedding. And in our family, premature births are the rule. Your own mama was only seven months when you were born, Jane. Such a puling wee thing, we were afraid we'd lose you. If this child doesn't go to full term—well, what would not Lady Sykes make of that? Probably have the child declared adulterine, and the estate snatched from him. If it's a male, I mean. That is what Pargeter was hoping for, of course. It is half the reason he married me. And half the reason I married him. It wasn't just the money and title and all this." She swept a careless arm around the saloon. "I would like to have a child. What lady wouldn't? I was not likely to get another chance at my age."

"I'm not condemning you. It's marvelous news. I just don't see why you make a secret of it. That gives it a questionable air. If you take care of yourself, there's no reason you should give birth prematurely."

"I can't conceal it much longer, but I'm not ready to announce it yet. With luck, Lady Sykes will be gone before my condition is noticed. You know how spiteful she is already. If she found out I'm carrying the future heir as well, I really don't know what the creature might do. Once she's back in London, she'll forget about me."

"Does Lord Malton know?"

"Oh yes. Pargeter went crowing to him the instant he suspected it. Malton has known all along, which made it harder that he didn't call on me. But we are fast friends now. In fact, he . . ." Jane gave her a questioning look. Lady Pargeter blushed and twiddled her fingers. "After it is over, Malton wants me to marry him."

"Good God! And will you have him?"

"Why not?" Fay asked in a challenging way. "And give him a son as well if I'm able."

Jane sat, temporarily bereft of speech. So many major changes occurring so quickly left her in a daze, but she did manage to hug her aunt's shoulders and murmur a few supportive platitudes. Her aunt, who had long kept her secrets locked in her bosom, welcomed the chance to talk. Her words came rushing out in a flood.

"If my child is a boy—that is why the full reading of the will was delayed a year, until we found out—then, of course, he will inherit Wildercliffe and the title. If it is a girl, I was to have the use of Wildercliffe during my lifetime, with, of course, a substantial dowry for our daughter. Now that I have settled with Malton, I shall remove to his estate and hand the running of Wildercliffe over to Harold Soames, with the income, of course, mine during my lifetime. Soames is to inherit when I die if the child is a girl, or in case I miscarry. At my age, there is no saying. Cassidy foresees no difficulty, however."

"And Nigel Sykes was never considered as the heir?"

"Only in his mama's head. He didn't expect it himself, or he would be here with her, stirring up a hornet's nest."

"Mr. Soames will be living at Wildercliffe, then, whether your child is a boy or girl?" This being the case, Jane was curious to learn something of him.

"I shall ask him to do it. I think he will agree. He lives in a rented house now—not very well-to-do, whatever Phoebe says—but a bright and honest man. He and his wife could live here. My son would be close enough that he could come often and be instructed by Soames in the running of the estate. Malton is too old to take the job on."

"I see," Jane said pensively. She soon realized that her present job was redundant in this arrangement. Aunt Fay wouldn't need a companion when she was married—but she would have a child to care for. "You'll need a nursemaid," she said hopefully.

Her aunt smiled. "We have decided you are to marry Swann, have we not?"

"Indeed we have not. I like him, but I don't love him."

"Oh, Jane!" her aunt said with a *tsk*. "Loving is not for such tenuous ladies as you and I. We must look out for our future. Where would I be today if I had refused Pargeter? I would be Mrs. Swann's companion—if I were lucky. There was some talk of it when Lady Pargeter died. The old lady needs a companion. And instead of that I am a baroness, fast on my way to becoming a countess. Where will you be ten years from now if you don't nab Swann? In some such spot at Miss Prism's Academy, or nursemaid for me. It is not to be thought of. Give up this foolish idea of romance and nab Swann, while you have the chance."

Jane knew the advice was sensible. It was no new thing for a young lady to marry without love in the hope that love would grow along with familiarity, but she could no more do it than she could allow Fortini to take liberties with her. To marry a man she didn't love . . . Even if there was no other gentleman a lady did care for, it would be difficult. At the back of her mind there hovered the beguiling image of Lord Fenwick, to make it not only difficult but impossible.

How had Fay married a gentleman she didn't love? Jane didn't believe for one moment that she had loved that old Tartar, Lord Pargeter. Perhaps a lifetime of servitude had driven her to it. She wasn't a servant now, though, and she had agreed to marry Malton, another aging, pompous gentleman.

Jane thought of Swann, who was neither aging nor pompous. In fact, she quite liked him. No, it was too high a price to pay for diamonds and a fancy house. When a woman sold her body, her freedom, her very spirit, were an integral part of the bargain. She renounced all hope of love, and twenty-three was too young an age to abandon a dream.

"I must do as I think best," Jane said, and drew the conversation back to her aunt's future. There was so much to discuss there that the talk went on for hours. Jane glanced at the ornate French clock on the mantel from time to time, thinking that Lord Fenwick might call, since he must be at loose ends at Swann Hall. At eleven no one had called, and the ladies retired.

The next morning they wrote the invitations for Lady Pargeter's dinner party. It was to consist of the same people who attended Mrs. Swann's party, except that Lord Malton would replace Mr. Parker, and of course, Mrs. Swann would not come. In the afternoon they delivered the invitations, using Lady Pargeter's elegant chaise. Their first stop was Swann Hall.

Jane had a sinking feeling she would learn that Lord Fenwick had left for his hunting box, but he was there when she was shown into the saloon. He looked up from his newspaper. When his dark eyes met hers, she was sure she saw a leap of pleasure there. A spontaneous smile flashed and lingered long enough to give her hope. Yet he hadn't come to call last night. He had nothing more pressing to do today than read the journals, but he didn't come to see her.

In the corner, Horace Gurney smiled the uncertain smile of a man in his cups, said, "Good day, Rampling," and lifted his glass to her.

"This is Lady Pargeter, Horace," his sister said with a commanding eye. When Lady Pargeter just shook her head, Phoebe knew any hope for a match between them was vain.

Lady Sykes and Lady Pargeter immediately began a verbal skirmish.

"No written reply is necessary," Fay said, handing her enemy the invitation. "So finicky, don't you think, to request a written reply for a simple dinner party? I wouldn't have bothered with the card, but I thought you might not be in this afternoon. I meant to leave it with Morton."

"That is your provincial upbringing speaking, my dear Lady Pargeter. In London we are always so full of invitations that we never give a verbal reply. We have to check our calendars. A written reply is de rigueur."

"When in Rome, Lady Sykes. I doubt your calendar is full to overflowing here in the country."

"True, there is no one to call on here." Then she added with great condescension, "Present company excepted, of course. *Ça va sans dire.*"

"One wonders that you remain so long away from your friends," Lady Pargeter said. "You are missing the Season."

Jane took a chair beside Fenwick. "Where is Mr. Swann today?" she asked, as he wasn't in the room.

"He's gone haring after a rumor of black swans some twenty miles away—left right after breakfast. He mentioned asking you to accompany him, but as he was carrying two large baskets on the roof of his carriage, he thought you might not enjoy the trip."

"And what are you doing to amuse yourself, Lord Fenwick?"

"Demmed little. I rode this morning."

"I enjoy riding," she said, thinking he might take the hint and invite her to join him the next time. In fact, she was a little offended that he hadn't invited her that morning. "My aunt has a lady's mount in her stable," she said.

"That's nice. Then you won't be bored to flinders," he replied rather stiffly. She sensed the constraint in him. He was much less forthcoming than usual. "Scawen should be back late this afternoon," he said. "No doubt he'll call on you this evening and let you know all about his outing."

"I hope you will accompany him, if you have nothing better to do," she said. It was as bold a speech as she had ever made to a gentleman, and her cheeks flushed with embarrassment at her own audacity, but she had to know if he had any interest in her at all.

"I should enjoy it," he said. Then he gave her a diffident look and added, "Actually, I have a deal of correspondence I ought to be writing."

She took it as a direct rebuff. "I see," she said. Her aunt was right. Lord Fenwick had no interest in her. It was his easy London manners that had led her astray. Caught between shame and anger, she had never felt so miserable in her life.

Fenwick saw her state, and had a good idea as to the reason for it. He liked Jane too much to hurt her.

"It won't do, you know, Miss Lonsdale," he said gently. How to proceed with this delicate task without hurting her? She had already stiffened noticeably. He'd mention Swann's fondness of her. "I am Swann's guest. It would be wrong of me to interfere in his romance."

Jane snatched at this face-saving crumb. "Oh, is that why you suddenly turned so cool after our drive? I must admit I did wonder if I had offended you."

"Jane," he said, shaking his head. "I shouldn't think you've ever offended anyone in your life. You're quite different from most ladies. So shy and gentle. You wouldn't believe what some young ladies get up to."

"What do you mean?" she asked with real interest.

There was a visit to be got in somehow, and he decided to amuse her with the story of Miss Merton, whose name he withheld like a gentleman.

"Well, to take one example, I am at present being pursued by a certain Miss X, who has hounded me from London to Brighton to Bath, and I have no doubt she is not far from my hunting box this minute, waiting for me. I feel like a fox running for cover."

"She's not the only one after you, I take it?"

"Certainly not. We well-to-do bachelors are prime targets for all the nubile ladies. You notice how modestly I disclaim that the ladies have any interest in my poor self. Well, I daresay the title helps, if that can be considered a part of myself."

"But don't you want to get married and settle down?" she asked. "I have always heard it is necessary when estates and titles are at stake."

"Certainly I do, but I prefer to make my own choice. I'll not be bullocked into it by a marauding female."

"Well, I never thought I should feel sorry for you, but I expect it is rather harrowing, pelting all over the countryside to escape entrapment."

"Yes, it was a great boon to me, finding this safe corner of the country, away from all the ladies."

Jane was accustomed to disappointments. She took this latest with her usual stoicism. She had always known Fenwick was above her touch, and she had now heard from his own lips that he had no interest in her. She was "safe"; there was no danger of his falling in love with her.

"If Miss X discovers you at your hunting box, you know where you will be safe," she said.

He frowned then, wondering if he hadn't made himself sound like a coxcomb. "I hope you don't think . . ."

"What?"

"Nothing."

The other conversation suddenly rose in volume. Jane heard the name Parker, and turned her attention to hear more.

"Not inviting Mr. Parker?" Lady Sykes was saying, with a tinge of annoyance.

"It would throw my table out of kilter. Four ladies and four gentlemen will do admirably for a small, informal dinner. I hope Mr. Gurney will come—if he is able."

Fay looked to the corner, where Horace was falling asleep, but he made the effort to smile and assure her he would attend.

"You have only three gentlemen," Lady Sykes pointed out. "Fenwick, Swann, and Gurney."

"Oh, did I not mention it? My good friend Lord Malton has accepted. I could not leave him out. He would take it very much amiss. We are bosom bows."

"Dear Malton," Lady Sykes said, with a shake of her head. "He is looking ancient since his wife died, is he not?"

"I've noticed a marked improvement since he has begun calling regularly on me," Fay replied.

Lady Sykes's sharp eyes snapped. She had had some thoughts of nabbing Malton herself, but he had not returned her one call. He had been such a lethargic host that she hadn't bothered to call again.

"Setting up a new beau, Lady Pargeter?" she inquired ironically. "In London society, it is the custom to wait until the crape is set aside before going courting."

"Lord Malton is not in mourning; it is he who is doing the courting."

Lady Sykes turned a fulminating eye on her brother. "Get Lady Pargeter a glass of wine, Horace. Where are your manners?"

"We must be leaving," Lady Pargeter said, rising. "We still have to call on Mrs. Rogers. We wanted to make sure you were free before inviting her."

"Of course I'm free. What else is there to do in the middle of nowhere?"

Horace knew Phoebe was annoyed with him, and struggled to his feet to accompany the ladies to the door, leaving Fenwick to receive the blast of Phoe-be's ire.

"You see what she is up to!" she said. "Poor old Pargeter still warm in his grave, and already she is legging it after another fortune! And the young chit was rolling her eyes at you, Fenwick. Watch your step, or you will be added to their harem."

A glint of anger flashed behind his smiling fa-cade. "What a slow top you are, Phoebe. You should have tossed your own bonnet at Malton."

"At least mine is not draped in crape."

She rustled from the room and went calling on Lord Malton within the half hour, only to learn he had gone to call on Lady Pargeter.

Chapter Fifteen

"I am going to call on Miss Lonsdale," Scawen announced after dinner that evening. "You'll come with me, Fen?"

"I have some correspondence I must write," Fenwick replied. "In fact, I shan't be able to remain with you any longer, Swann. I had a note from Mama this morning. I must go to Bath to tend to some business for her. Perhaps you will be kind enough to deliver this note to Lady Pargeter, begging off. She will want to find another man for her dinner table. I've written Miss Lonsdale a farewell note as well."

Swann accepted the notes reluctantly. "Dash it, how can I court Jane without you to oil the wheels for me? You will be coming back soon, I hope?"

"That's up to you, Swann. I shall return to stand as best man at your wedding, if you like."

"I'll never get her to the altar without you to give her a shove. She's always livelier when you're along."

Fenwick was aware of a keen desire to stay, but it would be wretched to take advantage of such a trusting soul as Swann.

"You'll do fine by yourself," Fenwick assured him.

Lady Sykes was happy to hear of Fenwick's

departure. At least he wasn't enamored with the schoolteacher. Phoebe had had no reply to her note to Nigel. No doubt he had gone rattling off to Newmarket to lose money on the horse races.

"Bath, you say?" Lady Sykes said to Fenwick. "Do give my regards to your dear mama, Fenwick. And while you are there, you might have a word with Miss Prism to check up on Miss Lonsdale. I've written a dozen lettters to Bath. No one has ever heard of her. I begin to wonder if she was ever there at all. Really, it is very mysterious."

Fenwick stiffened in annoyance. "Do your own dirty work, Lady Sykes."

"I'm not suggesting there is anything amiss with the girl personally," Lady Sykes assured him. "Who got the position for her, is all I mean. Who she received letters from—that sort of thing. I have been pondering this business of Lady Pargeter running after Malton. Why would she be so eager to nab another *parti* if she were sure of keeping Wildercliffe? Depend upon it, when the year is up, the estate will go to Miss Lonsdale, Pargeter's by-blow daughter."

"Why would Pargeter wait a year to establish his daughter, if Miss Lonsdale were his daughter? You're hunting mares' nests, Phoebe."

Phoebe said no more. The full depth of Fenwick's scheming had just occurred to her. He was dashing off to Bath for no other reason than to ascertain that Jane was the future owner of Wildercliffe, before rushing back to marry her. Her anxiety soared. She would send Mr. Parker to Bath to look into the matter for her, at once. He must make discreet queries at Radstock, too. If a Mrs. Lonsdale ever gave birth to a daughter, which she took leave to doubt, the church would have a record of it.

She sent a note off to Parker that very night. Knowing he had a position, she suggested that he say his mama was ill, to account for his absence from school. She was so eager for news that she offered the loan of her own carriage for the trip. She had little occasion to use it herself in any case. Parker was so eager to ingratiate a baronet's wife, and to have a free trip in a well-sprung carriage, that he leapt at the offer.

Fenwick, in his room writing letters, didn't hear Parker arrive at Swann Hall. Fenwick felt it was the proper thing for him to leave the field to Scawen, and he could not account for his reluctance to do it. As he sat with the pen in his fingers, staring at the empty page, he saw Jane's face floating at the edge of his mind. Her shy gaze, her trembling smile, brought an answering smile to his own lips. He remembered her pleasure in the marchpane, and what she called the "wonderful outing" to the village. What would she not say about London?

For quite thirty minutes he sat, imagining how she would look in better bonnets, only to find her low poke suited her best. He imagined how her blue eyes would grow in wonder when he showed her the sights of London. Had she ever been there? He didn't know. She hardly ever spoke of herself. Perhaps Swann would take her there on their wedding trip. His rueful smile dwindled to a frown. Swann wouldn't show her the things she would want to see. He'd sit home by the fire, spilling tea on his waistcoat and patting his dog.

He frowned the image away and drew the sheet forward. No doubt he would forget Miss Lonsdale and her trembling smile, once he was away. He would spend a day or two with Mama—long enough for Miss Merton to hear rumors that he was there—before slipping quietly off to Newmarket.

Scawen Swann was at Wildercliffe that same evening, having uphill work trying to entertain Miss Lonsdale, who was in the megrims to learn that Lord Fenwick was leaving Swann Hall before the dinner party, and without even coming to take his leave in person. She tried to find Mr. Swann amusing, but his mumbling and stumbling only increased her headache.

All she wanted to do was run up to her room and read again the brief note Swann had delivered. Ere long she excused herself and did just that.

"Dear Miss Lonsdale: I regret that business makes it necessary for me to leave for Bath early tomorrow morning. I shall not be able to attend the dinner party, to which I looked forward with so much pleasure. Kindest regards, your servant, Fenwick."

That was all. Not a word about hoping to meet her again. Nothing personal. He had written a similar note to Fay. Jane's only consolation was that he need not have written to her at all. At least he had taken that much trouble.

The next day it rained buckets. Jane went to the library, where she stared out the windows at the falling rain, which struck the windows with a hard slap, before trickling in rivulets down the glass. Rain turned the parkland into a silver haze, streaked with menacing shadows from the trees. She only emerged from the library for meals.

Lord Malton braved the elements to entertain Fay in the afternoon. The rain kept Scawen at home, for which Jane was grateful. On Friday she was busy with arrangements for the dinner party. She offered to oversee the table and the flowers, but knowing that Fenwick would not be of the party robbed her job of any real pleasure. What would Swann care for flowers?

The dinner party itself was an anticlimax. With Fenwick absent, the table was uneven. Jane had balked at learning that Fay had invited Mr. Parker to even the numbers. As it turned out, the footman who delivered the message was told that Parker was visiting his sick mama, so the incumbent vicar was invited to replace him. Reverend Hellman had turned the late Reverend Rogers's practices on their ear, lending the services a High Church touch of Rome that was unacceptable to Mrs. Rogers.

Between the ecclesiastical sniping and the verbal darts thrown between Fay and Phoebe and Mr. Swann's spilling a full glass of red wine on the tablecloth and Horace Gurney's bleary, wordless stare, the dinner party was declared a disaster. Jane tried to keep her spirits up for her aunt's sake. She told herself she was infinitely better off than she had been at Miss Prism's, yet the dull ache in her heart did not go away.

It was temporarily forgotten the next morning when Fay handed her a letter postmarked from Bath. Fenwick was the name that darted into her head, but as soon as she saw the elegant copperplate writing, she knew the letter was from Harriet. Fenwick wrote a bold, masculine fist.

News from Harriet was always of interest, however, and she read the letter eagerly.

"Oh dear!" she exclaimed a moment later.

"What is it, Jane?" her aunt asked in alarm.

"Harriet has been turned off. I wager Fortini has been at her since I left."

"The poor girl."

Jane read on quickly. Already it had darted into her head that her aunt might invite Harriet to Wildercliffe until she could find another position. The same thing had occurred to Harriet, and in fact, desperation had led her to take the unusual liberty of announcing that she would be arriving that same day. She was full of apologies. She promised she would not stay long and would be honored to find a cot in the servants' quarters for a night or two. She had nowhere else to go. She said she would be happy to earn her keep. Tears started in Jane's eyes to learn Harriet's predicament. She read the pathetic passage to her aunt, to soften her heart.

"She apologizes too much," was Lady Pargeter's comment. "Naturally she will come here, until we can find another place for her. Tell Broome to air the yellow guest room next to yours, Jane. You two will have a deal of gossip to catch up on. I shouldn't be surprised if Mrs. Swann could use her. She really needs a companion. You will be happy for Harriet's company when you are at the Hall, eh?" she suggested archly.

Preparing for Harriet's arrival helped to ease the pangs of losing Fenwick. Harriet came on the four-o'clock stage, and was met in Bibury by Jane in Lady Pargeter's carriage. Beneath an elegant, cool exterior, Miss Stowe had the heart of a rabbit. She was tall, with raven hair pulled severely back from a broad, high brow. Her aquiline nose lent her a forbidding air that led acquaintances to anticipate a much stronger character than the girl possessed.

After the young ladies had embraced and exchanged greetings and were settled in the carriage on their way to Wildercliffe, Harriet said, "What a handsome carriage, but you shouldn't have brought it just for me, Jane! What a dreadful nuisance I am. I'm so sorry."

"Never mind that. It was Fortini, wasn't it? I know it was!" Jane said. "What did he do?"

"Nothing. It was not Fortini."

"What happened, then?"

"Miss Prism had a caller yesterday—a young gentleman caller, asking questions about *you*, Jane. When I heard, I darted straight down to her office, hoping to get a look at Lord Fenwick, for he sounded charming in your letter."

"Lord Fenwick called on Miss Prism?"

"I assumed it was he. Who else would be inquiring for you? Miss Prism didn't say a word to a soul. You know what an oyster she is. Lord Fenwick didn't drive his yellow curricle with all the silver on it," Harriet continued. "He came in a very handsome black carriage. All the girls—the teachers, I mean—were talking about it. It was Lottie who told me he was inquiring about Miss Lonsdale. He actually told her that when he asked to see Miss Prism."

"Lord Fenwick did go to Bath yesterday," Jane said. The carriage sounded very much like Fenwick's traveling carriage. He would have taken it for the trip to Bath. "But why was he inquiring about me, I wonder?"

"Perhaps if he's planning to offer, he's checking up on you," Harriet said hopefully. "Of course, Miss Prism told him all about Fortini. Her version of it, I mean."

"Are—are you sure she told him about Fortini?" Jane asked. She was assailed by a thousand questions and doubts. The first shiver of excitement that Fenwick was thinking of offering for her was closely followed by annoyance that he felt it necessary to check up on her. Hard on the heels of annoyance came chagrin that he would hear such a distorted view of her character. He would think she had been throwing herself at the music teacher! Oh dear, and he had made fun of those ladies who hounded gentlemen.

"Oh, certainly. I loitered outside the door of her office, pretending I wanted to see her about Lady Alice deGrue. Lady Alice has stopped eating—again. Of course, she stuffs herself with sweets from home, but Miss Prism told me to let her know if Lady Alice was not cleaning her plate, so it made an excellent excuse."

"What did Miss Prism say?" Jane asked, yet she was loath to hear the answer.

"I couldn't hear everything she said—you know the way she lowers her voice when she's gossiping, but I definitely heard the words 'Fortini' and 'throwing herself at him' and 'lascivious behavior.' Lascivious, imagine! What does it mean? It sounds horrid."

"It *is* horrid."

"That would be why Lord Fenwick was so angry. He said he was shocked that Miss Prism would have such immoral teachers."

"Did he mean me or Fortini?"

Harriet paused to consider it. "I'm sorry, Jane. I don't know for certain, but Miss Prism would have put the whole mess in your dish."

"Of course she would."

"She will never see a flaw in *him*. I wanted to march right in and tell Miss Prism what I thought of her. Except that Lottie came along just then with the tea tray—Miss Prism served him tea. He stayed quite half an hour—so I had to get back to my class.

"I didn't see Lord Fenwick leave. I wish I could have got a look at him. However, I did go to speak to Miss Prism when my classes were over. I was so frightened my heart was banging against my ribs, but I could not let her get away with that. I told her it was Mr. Fortini who pestered all the teachers, and she ought to turn him off. I told her that Lord Fenwick was courting you, and if she thought she was doing herself any favors by slighting the lady he planned to marry, she was much mistaken."

"He is not courting me! Why did you say such a thing, Harriet?"

"I'm sorry, Jane. But in your letter, you said he called, and invited you out. You said he was charming. He gave you marchpane. Of course he is courting you."

"Oh dear! But at least you told Miss Prism that *after* Lord Fenwick had left? She could not have told him I said that."

"Yes, to be sure. And she said, 'Miss Lonsdale gives herself a great many airs, but it is news to me that she is a fine lady. She is nothing more than a penniless vicar's daughter.' And that angered me, for it was a jab at myself as well. Anyway, the upshot of it is that she told me I was overreaching my position to criticize her, and if I was so fond of Miss Lonsdale, perhaps I ought to join her at Wildercliffe. I said, 'Does that mean you are letting me go, Miss Prism?' And she said, 'For once you have understood, Miss Stowe.' Was that not horrid of her?"

Jane gave her friend's hand a reassuring squeeze. "I suppose you cried and implored her for sympathy?"

"I may have shed a tear," Harriet said, blotting at her moist eyes, "but I did not implore her. I went straight to my room and wrote to you, then went to the staging office and arranged my trip. She let me stay in my room overnight. That was well done of her, was it not?"

"Oh, very generous!" Jane said angrily.

"She might have put me out on the street. I don't know what I shall do if she gives me a bad character. I could not like to ask her about that, for she was in a rare pelter. Do you think I should write to her and apologize?"

"Apologize for telling the truth? Certainly not! Lady Pargeter will give you a character. Actually, there is a possibility of employment at a neighbor's house. An elderly lady, an invalid, could use a companion."

"Oh, Jane! You are the best friend in the world!" Harriet said, and threw her arms around her friend.

Harriet was overcome with wonder when the carriage turned in at Wildercliffe. "Oh my! Your aunt must be very rich!" she said. She went trembling through the high oak portals, to stare at the rose marble floors, and at Broome, the butler, who greeted her austerely. She called him *sir*, and thanked him twice. She was so grateful to Lady

Pargeter that she was soon weeping copiously, and had to excuse herself to run up to her room to wash her face.

"Good Lord," Fay said to Jane. "One feels ill to see what a life of bondage does to a lady. Miss Stowe is a handsome gel, if she could only leave off weeping and striking her breast."

"She is shy," Jane said, "but she's honest, and a good worker, Aunt Fay."

"She would do very well for Mrs. Swann."

Jane didn't tell her aunt about Fenwick's visit to Miss Prism's Academy. If he had ever had any intention of offering for her, he wouldn't do it now that Miss Prism had blackened her character, so it was best to forget it. It rankled that he had been checking up on her. That was not the act of a man in love. Nor was that cold note he had written. Why would he be considering an offer if he didn't love her? She had no fortune, no position in society. Was it possible Harriet was mistaken about the man who had called on Miss Prism? But who else could it be, a young gentleman in a handsome carriage? Her mind was still brooding on this when she went up to change for dinner.

Chapter Sixteen

Scawen came to call after dinner. He took one look at the tall lady with the daunting face who sat beside Jane and feared his wooing would make no progress that evening. Miss Stowe was exactly the sort of lady who frightened him to death. She never smiled, she gave serious replies to any foolish comment he made. As soon as Lady Pargeter realized why he had become uncomfortable, she invited Harriet to sit with her and help her work the fire screen on which she was engaged. Harriet proved quite a dab at this pastime. She was always happiest when she was put to work. Fay informed her that it was Mr. Swann's mama who required a companion, and while they worked quietly, she gave Harriet some idea of the family's background.

Swann was then free to plod on with his courting. "I had no luck getting hold of the black swans from George Abernathy," he said. "After pelting all the way to Radstock, they turned out to be white swans after all. Not a black one in the batch. I am thinking of buying some dye and dying Darby and Joan."

"You were at Radstock?" Jane asked, interested to hear this had been his destination. "That is where I am from, Mr. Swann."

"I know. I had a look at the vicarage where you was born, Miss Lonsdale. A dandy little house, very cozy. I can just picture you there. I met the vicar, a Mr. Wodehouse. Seemed a nice chap. I was going to ask you to go with me, but it would have been no pleasure for you had I been carrying home a pair of swans. You have to go at a slug's pace to keep them calm."

"I would like to have gone," she said wistfully.

"Would you, by Jove? Then we shall go another time. Any time you like. Is there some special reason you have to go? Wodehouse told me someone had been inquiring for a copy of your birth from the parish register. I would have been happy to get it for you. You have only to ask, any little errands like that. Always happy to oblige."

"But I didn't send anyone on such an errand," she said, astonished to hear his story. He had surely got it wrong. Swann had said he knew Miss Lonsdale, and Wodehouse had mentioned someone else who was after a birth certificate. "Are you quite sure it was me he was talking about?"

Swann wrinkled his forehead up like a washboard. "There ain't another Miss Lonsdale from Miss Prism's Academy, is there? I had a few words with Wodehouse. When I mentioned you were here with your aunt, he asked if you had left Miss Prism's school. He knew who we were talking about right enough."

"And that is when he told you someone had been inquiring after me?"

"They were the very next words that left his mouth. 'Odd you should mention Miss Lonsdale,' he said. 'A gentleman was inquiring after her this very day.'"

"I wonder who it could have been."

"I wager Phoebe has a finger in it somewhere. It would be this foolish notion she has got into her head that you're Pargeter's by-blow. I wager she sent Nigel to check up on you. She's been sending out summonses to him all week, trying to reel him in to make a run at you. She fears you'll inherit the whole estate when the year is up. It ain't true, is it?" he asked with a scowl.

Jane stared in disbelief. "That I am Pargeter's illegitimate daughter?" she asked. "Of course not! Where did she get such a ridiculous notion?"

"Daresay it was the will not being read for a year, and you landing in on Rampling—that is, your aunt—at this time. Phoebe thinks Pargeter arranged it, to introduce you to the local society, and see how you go on. Something of the sort."

Jane laughed out loud, more in shock than amusement. "That's ridiculous! I know who my parents are. I have an ivory miniature of my mama. I look very much like her."

"Yes, but it ain't your mama she's worried about. It's your papa. He was the one with the blunt, you see. If he was Pargeter, I mean."

"My father was a simple vicar. This farouche story is all in Lady Sykes's head."

"That's what I thought," Swann said, happy to learn his intended wasn't a dashed heiress.

Jane was far from satisfied. Since she knew the real reason for the odd terms of the will, she didn't for one instant believe she was Lord Pargeter's daughter. She did want to discuss the matter with her aunt, however.

To arrange it, she said to Swann, "Would you not like to have a few words with Harriet? She is looking for a position. We thought your mama might want to hire her. Harriet is a very honest and conscientious worker."

"*Me* talk to her?" he asked, aghast.

"You won't be too firm, Mr. Swann? She's very shy."

"She don't look it. Why would she be shy of me?"

"If you hire her, then you would be her employer. She will be concerned for the impression she's making. We shan't mention her working for you this evening. Just meet her, and see if you think she would do."

Swann had a difficult time getting his mind around such an odd notion as that great ladder of a girl being frightened of him, but he wanted to please Jane. He agreed to talk to Miss Stowe.

He could sense her discomfort as soon as she was seated at his side. He set himself the task of putting her at ease, and decided after ten minutes that she was a pretty good sort of girl. Once she relaxed and learned how to smile, she'd do very well with his mama. Swann's vanity was so minuscule as to be nearly nonexistent, but what there was of it thrived under her deferential manner. She was as easily pleased as a puppy. She smiled at any little joke, and said he must think her very stupid when she thought a pen was a pen, and not a female swan.

Jane took up the needle Harriet had abandoned. While she plied it, she told her aunt about the man who had been making inquiries of her at Radstock. "Swann thinks it was Nigel. Phoebe thinks I am Pargeter's love child."

Fay gave a deep chuckle. "I wonder what put that bee in her bonnet. The strange will, I expect.

She would certainly send for Nigel if she thought you were the heir to Wildercliffe, though she mentioned the other day that she hadn't heard from him, and thought he must be at Newmarket. It's surely her doing. No one else would be so nosy."

Tea was served half an hour later. Swann managed a private word with Jane over the teacups.

"I think your Miss Stowe will do very well for Mama," he said. "I didn't mention it to her—you said not to—but I think she'll do."

"Oh, I am glad, Mr. Swann." Jane unthinkingly reached out and squeezed his fingers in gratitude. Swann latched on to them and squeezed back until her bones ached.

"Dash it, Miss Lonsdale, no matter if she was a Tartar, I'd hire her if it would please you."

Jane saw the gleam of passion in his eyes. "Oh!" she gasped, and withdrew her fingers. "You mustn't do it on my account, Mr. Swann."

"Can't you call me Scawen? I would like to call you Jane."

"It's a little early for that, Mr. Swann."

He took it as a promise of future intimacies, and said, "I hope you won't make me wait too long."

He enjoyed a good tea. As he rode home, he felt his romance was on the boil. He couldn't have done better if Fenwick had been there to egg him on.

After he left, Harriet admitted that she had found Mr. Swann most kind and interesting, and she hoped she had not made such a horrid impression on him that he had taken her in dislike.

"I don't think you need worry about that," Jane said.

The ladies decided to call at Swann Hall the next day to allow Harriet the opportunity to view her future home. While they chatted about Swann Hall, Jane's mind was full of her own problems. She didn't plan to tell Fay that Fenwick had been inquiring for her at Miss Prism's. That was her own private shame. Nor did she want to tell Harriet Phoebe's suspicions regarding her birth. Each of the ladies only knew half the story.

It was not until she was alone in her bedchamber that Jane could get down to serious brooding. She felt the two incidents were connected. It was beyond the realm of reason that two gentlemen should be inquiring about her at the same time. The obvious connection was that both Fenwick and Nigel were interested in courting her. Nigel because he thought she might inherit a fortune, and Fenwick because ... A heaviness began to creep over her spirits as realization dawned. If Phoebe had discussed this notion that she was Pargeter's daughter and heir, then Fenwick would have heard it. Was that why he had shown some interest in her? Was that why he had gone haring off to Miss Prism's to look into her character? She felt in her bones that it was.

Soon a worse realization took hold of her. Fenwick was in Bath, not ten miles from Radstock. It was Fenwick who had been inquiring regarding her birth! "A gentleman" was what Swann had said. He hadn't seen the man, or given any description of him. Fenwick was vetting her. He had gone to Miss Prism's first. Even the wretched account Miss Prism had given him wasn't enough to deter him if she were to inherit Wildercliffe. He was nothing else but a fortune hunter—and here she had thought him something quite out of the ordinary.

What did she know about him, after all? Not all noblemen were rich. He might be a gambler in debt to his ears; he might be a womanizer. He might be any dreadful thing, behind that handsome, smiling mask of the gentleman. The first time she had seen him he had been snooping around Lord Pargeter's room. He had only come here to see if he could make mischief. Well, he had made plenty—and much good it did him. He couldn't break the will, and he wasn't going to nab an heiress. She gave her anger full rein. She had every reason to be angry with him, and no reason at all to feel the sad regret lurking beneath the anger, because he had never really cared for her.

His teasing and joking were only to keep her in curl until he found out whether she was an heiress. That was why he had written that note. It suggested interest without in any way compromising him, if what he learned at Radstock didn't fit in with his plans. Now that he knew she was only a humble vicar's daughter, she would never see him again. That should have been some relief, but it only increased the ache in her heart.

Chapter Seventeen

Jane wished she could stay home the next morning when the ladies were preparing for the visit to Swann's, but she knew Fay would dislike it. A companion did as her mistress wished, even when her mistress was also her aunt. Perhaps it wouldn't be so bad to be married to Swann after all. He would be easy to manage, and at least she would be her own mistress.

A smiling Scawen met them at the door. He complimented both the younger ladies on their bonnets. Jane noticed that Harriet blushed up to her eyes and said that it was most obliging of him, as her bonnet was aeons old.

"It just suits you," he said. Even this ambiguous remark Miss Stowe took with a smile.

Harriet was introduced to Lady Sykes, who subjected her to a close scrutiny and a barrage of questions. Mr. Gurney had not yet arisen. Phoebe sat alone, her eyes glittering with suppressed excitement. She refrained from battle until she had established exactly who Harriet was.

Before long, Scawen said, "I thought you might like to take a hike upstairs to meet Mama, Miss Stowe. She is expecting you. She always likes to meet any new callers."

"That is very kind of you," Harriet said, rising to follow him from the saloon, murmuring, "Excuse me" and "Sorry" to left and right as she departed.

Jane heard Harriet demurring and Swann reassuring her as he led her toward the stairs. "I am so nervous, Mr. Swann."

"Nothing to be nervous about, my girl. She won't bite you. Even if she did, she's missing half her teeth."

Once they had left, Lady Sykes sat like a poisonous adder, primed to spit venom at her victims.

"Well, Miss Lonsdale," she said, wriggling in anticipation of the ammunition she had to pummel the enemy. "So you have brought a teaching friend to join you at Wildercliffe. Why was Miss Stowe turned off? Not for carrying on with the music master, I hope? Such a forward creature would not do for Mrs. Swann's companion."

Phoebe's snapping eyes, even more than her barbed words, revealed that she knew the story of Fortini. It was no hypothetical "music master" to whom she referred.

"No, she was dismissed for defending my fair name when Miss Prism unjustly accused me of misbehavior."

"Unjustly?" Phoebe laughed ironically. "Miss Prism has a sterling character. She hasn't the reputation of accusing anyone *unjustly*. Her school is most highly regarded, which makes it imperative that she not have women of loose morals teaching her girls."

Lady Pargeter took up her cudgel with a fulminating eye. "She is less stringent in her requirements of her male teachers," she said. "For your information, Lady Sykes, the music master made improper advances to Miss Lonsdale."

"A likely story!"

"It is of no interest to Miss Lonsdale or myself whether you choose to believe it or not, but it happens to be true," Fay said grandly. "As a matter of curiosity, might I know how you came to be aware of all this?"

"You can't hope to keep a scandal like that quiet for long! I wager Bath is humming with it by now. I wonder what Lady Fenwick will make of it."

"That is of no more interest to us than what you think of it, Lady Sykes," Fay retaliated.

Phoebe turned a disparaging eye on Jane. "You want to keep on your aunt's good side, Miss Lonsdale, for you will never find any other position with the sort of reference Miss Prism will give you."

"My niece is not looking for another position," Fay shot back. "I wouldn't part with her for any consideration."

Jane felt a pronounced desire to flee the room, but until Harriet returned, she must sit and be insulted. She hadn't the heart to defend herself, nor was it necessary. Aunt Fay could and did do a much better job of it.

After a deal of gibing and verbal sparring, Swann's heavy tread was heard on the staircase. He and Harriet duly appeared in the saloon.

"What, no tea?" Swann said, looking around.

"Lady Sykes and I have been having such an interesting conversation, she forgot to order it," Lady Pargeter said.

Swann said, "I'll do it this instant."

"Not on our account, Mr. Swann," Fay said, rising.

"I have quite lost my appetite, and I am sure my niece feels the same," she said, with a disparaging glance at Phoebe. "Miss Stowe, are you ready to leave?"

"Certainly, milady," Harriet said. "Sorry to have kept you waiting."

Swann accompanied the ladies to the doorway. "I am taking Harriet to see the swans this afternoon," he said to Jane. "I hope you'll come with us."

"Thank you, I have seen the swans," Jane said in a weak voice. She only wanted to go home and forget this awful visit.

"There will soon be some new ones for you to see. Had a letter from Fenwick this morning. He has got a line on a black pair for me."

Jane waited on tenterhooks to hear if he had anything further to say about Fenwick. She bit back the nearly overwhelming urge to ask. Swann immediately spoke of other things, arranging a time to call for Harriet.

The conversation on the drive home was about Harriet's meeting with Mrs. Swann.

"She seemed to like me," Harriet said shyly. "Mr. Swann is sure she will hire me. He didn't like to ask her in front of me, you know, but he feels she will have me. Is it not fortunate, Jane? We shall be neighbors, and Mr. Swann is so considerate, I'm sure he won't object to my calling on you. He says his mama usually sleeps the afternoon away."

"That is good news," Jane said. She had to force herself to simulate enthusiasm, for her mind was elsewhere.

Swann had heard from Fenwick. That was how Lady Sykes knew all about her disgrace. Fenwick had sat right down and written all the details of his investigation to that dreadful woman. Probably warned her not to send for Nigel, now that they knew she was penniless. The frustration grew in Jane until she wanted to haul off and strike someone.

"And of course, you will call on me," Harriet said. "Mr. Swann says I can have the use of his carriage when he is not using it, and the donkey cart any time I like, as soon as he gets it painted, and gets a donkey."

"He is very considerate," Jane said.

She was too upset to notice that Scawen was showing Harriet all the consideration he used to lavish on her, nor would she have cared a groat if she had noticed, except to be happy for Harriet.

Swann came immediately after lunch to take Harriet to see the swans. Malton arrived half an hour later. As the day was so fine, he invited Lady Pargeter out for a drive.

"You come with us, Jane," Lady Pargeter said.

Jane was happy to have a while to herself. "I would prefer to take a walk about the estate," she said. "I need some exercise."

"You do look a little peaky," Malton said at once. Jane sensed that Malton wanted his lady to himself.

As soon as they left, she took up a novel and strolled out into the park. She had no intention of reading, but the book made a good excuse to sit under a tree on a balmy day and think. Her first thoughts were of Fenwick's perfidy. This was so painful that she forced her mind into the future. Her situation wasn't desperate by any means. Her aunt would never turn her off. She could be useful during Fay's confinement, and afterwards help with the baby. She had no experience of infants, but it couldn't be so difficult. Women had a natural instinct to care for children. There would be a wet nurse, of course, to tend to the feeding and help out.

Before too many years, Malton would be too old to get about. He was considerably older than Fay, and not in the best of health. At least he complained a good deal. Then Fay would be happy to have a companion. And if her child was a girl, she would require a governess. There Jane felt she could make a real contribution.

Was that to be her future, attaching herself like a barnacle to her aunt, living vicariously through Fay? Growing old in another lady's house, that dread creature the poor relation? Worst of all, the spinster. It was almost as dreary as teaching at Miss Prism's. The physical amenities were superior, of course, but at least at the school she had been living her own life, not someone else's.

The ultimate irony was that she faced this bleak future because Mr. Fortini had found her attractive. He was "overcome by her ravishing beauty," he had said. It was what he said to all the ladies he molested. Odd he was never overcome by the ravishing beauty of the noble daughters he taught. Their pedigree protected them from such licentious behavior. Miss Prism might turn a blind eye to the complaints of her teachers, but not of her pupils.

Jane looked up when she heard the sound of a horse approaching, expecting to see only the bailiff or game warden. She gave an instinctive gasp of surprise tinged with pleasure when she recognized Lord Fenwick. The sight of him in Pargeter's meadow, mounted on a sleek bay mare, threw her into temporary confusion. Even while her stomach tightened in anger, she noticed how handsome he looked, how well he sat his mount, as if born in the saddle. No wonder she had fallen in love with him. He should be riding a white steed, girded in gold. He might be a prince riding out of a fairy tale, with the blue sky and green meadow around him and the sun forming a halo against his head and broad shoulders.

How dare he come here after prying into her life, causing trouble? She was overcome with a blind rage. Here was the cause of half her woes. The little scandal might have died aborning if he had not gone to Bath, digging into it all. Lady Sykes would be bound to trumpet the story around Bibury, causing Jane's potential friends to despise her. She rose up from the grass, rigid in her fury, as if she were meeting an armed adversary. The final straw was that he tried to con her with a smile.

"Miss Lonsdale, what luck to find you alone. I was just on my way to call on you." He dismounted in an easy glide, holding on to the reins.

Jane found she could hardly speak for the tightness in her throat and the pounding in her breast. "What do you want now?" she demanded in an angry, strained voice that she hardly recognized.

A playful frown drew Fenwick's eyebrows together. "Get up on the wrong side of the bed this morning, Miss Lonsdale?" he asked.

"Why didn't you stay away? Why did you have to come back?"

"Why do you think, Jane?" he asked softly, and reached his arms out to her. The way he spoke, using her Christian name, had a devastating effect on her taut nerves.

The scene was so different from what she expected that she hardly knew how to respond. Instead of the haughty contempt she expected to see on his face, she saw only confusion, rapidly changing to a warm smile as their gazes held. Before she could draw back, his arms were around her, cradling her gently against his shoulder.

"Tell me all about it, my dear," he murmured. "This hostility is not like my gentle Jane. Who has been annoying you?"

She drew back and looked up at him with a question in her eyes. That "my dear" sounded like celestial chimes in her ears. What new mischief was he contriving against her with his insidious charm? "Yes, someone has been pestering me! You! Why did you do it? Why did you go to Bath?"

The small smile that curved his lips rose slowly to light his eyes as she watched, mesmerized. "You missed me? Good! I missed you, too, more than I would have thought possible. I haven't slept a wink for thinking of you, Jane," he said, and lowered his head to kiss her.

Jane's heart trembled in tune with her lips. When he firmed her lips with his kiss, her heart trembled the harder and her knees turned to water. The warmth of his body seeped into hers in a thrilling intimacy she had never even imagined, disarming her hostility. His arms tightened insensibly until he was crushing her against the hard wall of his masculinity. It was like a dream, washing away all the doubts and fears and anger that had engulfed her. He had missed her! He must care for her, at least a little. For a full minute she succumbed to the madness, before sanity returned.

What was he doing? Why was he making love to

her? He knew she was a penniless orphan—and he imagined she was a loose woman. That was it! He thought he could play fast and loose with her because of her imagined scarlet past. A lady who gave herself to a music master would be easy prey to a handsome lord. That was what he thought of her, that she was free for the taking, like a lightskirt. She wrenched from his arms and glared at him.

"If I were a man, I'd run you through," she said, through clenched teeth. The frustration of the past days boiled over to temporary madness. She could hardly see his face for the scalding tears that pooled in her eyes when she lifted her hand and struck him a sharp blow across the cheek. Caught off guard, he reeled back from the force of the blow and stood rubbing his cheek and breathing hard while he got his anger under control.

"You had only to say if you didn't want me to kiss you," he said stiffly.

"You didn't ask, milord. Odd that didn't occur to you, when you are so fond of asking questions!"

"What is that supposed to mean?"

"You can forget what Miss Prism told you. I did not encourage Mr. Fortini. He molested me, as he molested countless other schoolmistresses."

Fenwick became perfectly rigid, just before he made a convulsive motion toward her. "*What! Who* molested you?" he demanded, fire in his eyes.

"I think you know who I am referring to. And you know as well that I am not Pargeter's daughter. I won't inherit a sou in the infamous will, Lord Fenwick, so I can only assume you are after me for some other purpose."

"What are you talking about, Jane?"

"About your trip to Bath. Sorry it was in vain.

And so was your inferior attempt at seduction. And now, if you will excuse me, I must leave."

His hand reached out and snatched her wrist. "Not without an explanation!"

She met his gaze defiantly. "You have misjudged your quarry, milord. Don't believe all you hear. Your trip to Radstock should have taught you that much."

She wrenched her wrist free and stalked at a stately pace off through the park, back to Wildercliffe, with the hot tears falling on her cheeks.

Fenwick mounted his mare and rode back to where he had seen Scawen with some lady. Perhaps Scawen could shed some light on what Jane had been talking about, this Fortini fellow. If he had molested Jane, he'd call him out. But why was she so angry with himself? Was it because he had left without saying good-bye? He knew before he was halfway to Bath that he would be back. Scawen hadn't offered for Jane. He had only known her a short while. Swann would find someone else. Jane's happiness was more important, and he felt in his bones that she loved him.

Fenwick had searched for and found a pair of black swans as a consolation prize for Swann. And while he was away, someone had driven Jane Lonsdale mad. Worse, that someone had turned her against him.

Chapter Eighteen

Jane was thankful to be alone when she returned to the house. She ran up to her room and threw herself on her bed to relive those agonizing moments with Fenwick. Every word he had uttered was indelibly etched on her heart. As she considered them in the relative calm of privacy, she realized his words and reactions were at odds with those of a guilty man. He had seemed confused by her accusation. What if the man at Miss Prism's hadn't been him? And the man at Radstock? But who else could it have been—a young gentleman in a handsome carriage?

If it hadn't been Fenwick, she had made a wretched botch of her future happiness. His manner, when he approached her, had been that of a lover. If he didn't think she was a fallen woman, then his behavior could only mean he had come to offer for her. And she had accused him of villainy; she had even struck him. What must he think of her? At the bottom of her misery, there was one small bubble of hope. It was the way he had smiled at her, the way he had called her "my Jane" and kissed her. Such love couldn't be lost because of a misunderstanding—could it?

Hope gave her courage to dry her eyes, wash her

face, and tidy her gown. She was more or less presentable when Harriet came tapping at her door half an hour later. Harriet came in hesitantly.

"I met Lord Fenwick," she said. "He's very handsome, Jane, but not an even-tempered gentleman. What did you say to him to put him in such a pucker?"

"You saw him! What did he say?"

"He said he was going to beat the dickens out of Fortini, after I told him—I'm sorry! Should I not have told him? He already knew Fortini's name, though he didn't seem to know quite who he was, which makes one wonder if Lord Fenwick was ever at Miss Prism's. Mr. Swann thinks it must have been Mr. Parker who was asking questions about you there. He said Lady Sykes was curious to learn all about you, and very likely that is why her carriage and team were missing from the stable that day, because she lent them to Parker. Mr. Swann is very clever at figuring things out. Perhaps Parker was the man at Radstock as well. Mr. Swann told me all about it. I hope you don't mind."

"It seems my life is an open book," Jane said.

"So romantic, being the daughter of a lord and a great heiress. It is quite like a novel. You must be almost sorry it isn't true."

Jane let Harriet ramble on while she considered what she had just heard. Of course, it had been Mr. Nosy Parker at Bath, sent by Lady Sykes to check up on her, before throwing Nigel at her head. And she had accused Fenwick without a shred of evidence, with nothing but her vile imagination to egg her on.

When Harriet stopped, Jane said, "I'm not sure

heiresses have it as easy as we always imagined, Harriet. Did Lord Fenwick seem very angry?"

"Furious."

"Oh dear. You mean furious at—at me?"

"At the whole world. He even kicked a swan, but not very hard. It was pulling at his coattails. Mr. Swann said it was looking for food in his pockets. Mr. Swann feeds them seeds and things."

"Oh." Jane saw that Harriet was more interested in Mr. Swann than in Lord Fenwick's fit of temper. As Harriet had run out of news, Jane said, "I expect we had best dress for dinner."

Harriet immediately headed for the door. Jane called after her, "Are they—is Mr. Swann calling this evening?"

"Yes, Mr. Swann said he would call after dinner. Lord Fenwick didn't say he would come with him. Don't worry, Jane. I don't think he will," she said supportively. "He was really very angry."

Harriet quietly closed the door and slipped away to change for dinner. She wished with all her heart that she had a nicer gown to wear for Mr. Swann. She was an extremely modest creature, but it was beginning to dawn on her that Mr. Swann did not find her unattractive, and if she could increase his interest, he might even offer marriage. She wished Jane could be equally fortunate, but she did not consider winning the affection of the violent-tempered Lord Fenwick anything but a calamity.

When the girls were on their way downstairs to dinner, both dressed in their best gowns, Jane asked Harriet not to mention anything about Fenwick to Lady Pargeter. "For it will only cause a commotion while we are eating, and that isn't good for my aunt in her condition."

"What condition? Is she ill? Oh dear, I'm sorry. I shouldn't be here if she's not well."

"No, not ill exactly."

"You don't mean—surely she cannot be enceinte!"

"Don't mention that either. It was supposed to be a secret."

"There are a great many secrets at Wildercliffe," Harriet said, but in no condemning way. In fact, she was rosy with pleasure. This whole visit was like a marvelous holiday to her. She couldn't stop smiling.

Mr. Swann did indeed arrive almost before they had left the table. His excuse was to announce that Lady Sykes was leaving in the morning and Fenwick had already left. Jane's hopes plummeted to hear the latter.

"Both gone darting off on me," he said. "Fenwick to Bath and Phoebe to London to catch the rest of the Season. By Jove, I am glad you are coming to us, Miss Stowe, or we would be lonesome as lobsters. Phoebe said to say her *au revoirs* for her and all that, Lady Pargeter. Oh, she sent you this note."

Swann handed Lady Pargeter a card bearing all of two lines. "Dear Lady Pargeter: Leaving tomorrow. Can't miss the Duchess of Portland's party. Sorry I can't call in person to say good-bye. Best wishes, Lady Sykes."

"She don't expect a reply," he said. "Said there was no use expecting one from a house—from you. Expect she meant you were too busy."

"She is quite right. I'm always too busy to write to her." Goaded on by that boasting mention of a duchess, Fay added, "I do have a verbal message, however. You can tell her I am sorry she won't be here for my wedding to Lord Malton. The nuptials will occur early in the new year, as soon as I get my figure back after my confinement."

Swann's jaw dropped. "Eh?" He lifted a finger and poked it about in his ear. "Thought you said something about a confinement."

"I did, Mr. Swann."

Swann turned quite pink with embarrassment. "None of my affair, to be sure, but why wait until the new year if you're—er—in that condition?"

"Lord Pargeter is my child's father."

"But he's dead!"

"So he is," Lady Pargeter said, and rang the bell for tea, even if it was too early.

Swann went into a conference with Harriet over these strange goings-on. At the embroidery frame by the grate, Lady Pargeter lifted an eyebrow at her niece and said, "You realize you've lost Swann to your friend?"

"I know it. They have my blessing. It's a match made in heaven."

"Perhaps he wasn't quite right for you. I believe he and Harriet will deal extremely well. Now, if we could only find a gentleman for you, Jane—"

Even as she spoke, there was a knock on the front door. Within seconds, Lord Fenwick was shown in. His elegant black jacket, starched white cravat, and the sparkling diamond in it were at dreadful odds with the black eye that stood out like a beacon.

"Lord Fenwick! What has happened to you?" Jane exclaimed, rising without realizing she did it when he entered.

"One assumes Lord Fenwick bumped into a door," Lady Pargeter said to her niece. "Is that not the usual cause of a gentleman's black eye, Fenwick?"

"Exactly," Fenwick said. "Doors are becoming entirely too aggressive this season." He greeted the assembled party with an exquisite bow.

"We hardly expected you back so soon," Lady Pargeter said in a questioning way. "Swann was just telling us you had gone to Bath."

She noticed that, although he was ostensibly speaking to herself, his eyes kept sliding to Jane. She noticed, too, the small smile lifting Jane's lips. Ere long, she figured out what was afoot, and a deep happiness seized her. So that was the way the land lay! She shouldn't be surprised. If she, at her age, could nab two lords, why should Jane not nab one? Fay soon excused herself on the pretext of seeing what was keeping the tea tray. She could give the young couple thirty minutes to reach an understanding without breaching the proprieties.

Fenwick didn't waste a minute. With an impatient glance at Swann and Harriet, he rose and put his hand out to Jane. "There is a book waiting for us in the library, Miss Lonsdale," he said.

She went nervously. When they were in the hallway he said, "Well, aren't you going to ask me how the other door is?"

"How is he? And who is he? Is it Mr.—"

"Mr. Parker, unfortunately, bumped into *two* doors. He looks charming in black, the scoundrel. I had to beat someone, and Phoebe, unfortunately— well, she is *called* a lady."

He opened the library door, showed her in, and closed the door behind them. A pair of lamps glowed on either side of the grate. The elongated shadows of the young couple rose up the walls of books and bent onto the ceiling, as if they were giants.

"I think I've figured out what happened," he said, holding tightly on to both her hands. "Miss—what is her name? Swann's new lady?"

"You mean my friend Harriet Stowe?"

"That's the one. She told me about Fortini, the wretch. If I'd known that when I was in Bath, I would have given him a taste of the home-brewed as well. In fact, I was halfway there to do it—well, I had gone two miles anyway—when I decided I had to see you first."

"You have my blessing. Give him a poke for me while you're about it."

"Are you sure you want me to do that?"

She looked a trifle miffed. "Are you suggesting I encouraged his advances?"

"Now, don't poker up on me, my sweet idiot. I am saying that if he hadn't kissed you, you wouldn't have left Miss Prism's and come here, and I would probably never have met you. As for encouragement, I doubt you were aware of the encouragement you gave. Parker tells me the man was overwhelmed by your ravishing beauty."

"Parker actually spoke to Fortini? Is there no end to his interference?"

"Apparently not, but you blame the messenger, in a manner of speaking. His orders from General Sykes were to glean any and all particulars of Lord Pargeter's by-blow. If he'd gone to Radstock first, he could have saved himself a deal of effort. Once he learned you're legitimate, his job was done."

"I feel like a criminal with all this investigating."

"Ah it's a hard fate to be a ravishing beauty, inciting men to forget themselves."

"That was only Fortini's excuse to kiss me."

"And how did he kiss you? Was it a salacious kiss? I may still have to go to Bath and trounce him."

"Good gracious, how should I know what it was? I'm no expert."

"You certainly fooled me," he said, with a rakish smile lighting his eyes as his arms went around her. "Did he kiss you like—this?" he said, and drew her close against him to ravage her with a soul-destroying embrace, until her heart was pounding in her ears and her lungs felt as if they would burst. His warm fingers massaged the vulnerable nape of her neck, before moving to her back to crush her against him.

"N-no, it was nothing like that," she said, when he finally released her.

For a long moment they stood, just gazing at each other in silence. Then Jane lifted her fingers to his cheek. "I'm sorry, Fenwick—about the meadow. What must you think of me?" she said in a small voice.

He took her hand and lifted it to his lips. "I think you are the most darling, adorable wretch who ever slapped my face. I thought you had run mad—or I had—or the whole demmed world had," he said, with a frown growing between his eyes. Then it eased to a soft smile. "Perhaps what I mean is that I thought you were miffed with me for leaving so suddenly, without calling. I did think your annoyance a tad excessive, but grand passions breed the grand gesture. It was that casual mention of a certain Fortini molesting you that made me realize there was more to it than anger at my desertion."

"I thought you mistook me for a lady of easy virtue."

He shook his head ruefully. "Never that. A blind man could see your virtue is unblemished."

He went to the sofa and drew her down beside him. "Did you really think I was checking up on you, Jane? I didn't want to go. I just felt I owed Swann the chance. He doesn't meet many ladies, and I knew you liked him. But then I thought of *your* feelings. I was arrogant enough to think perhaps you would prefer me to Scawen. By the time I had rationalized myself into thinking I was doing the right thing to come back, I was halfway to Bath, so I decided to continue on and tell Mama."

She listened, her joy rising at every word. But all she said was, "Tell her what?"

"That I am engaged. That is, I hope to be—if you'll have me."

"I shan't be inheriting Wildercliffe. I'm not Pargeter's daughter."

"I believe you're confusing me with your erstwhile long-distance suitor, Sir Nigel Sykes. And how dare you suggest I'm marrying you for your money!"

"I haven't said I'd marry you at all."

"You've lost out on Swann, and after I went to the bother of finding a pair of black swans to replace you."

A familiar smile trembled on her lips. "I couldn't possibly, Fenwick."

"My fiancées call me Desmond."

"I wouldn't know how to behave in the august society you inhabit."

"Behave like the lady you are—sane, sensible,

seductive. That last only when we are alone, of course."

"Seductive!"

"In your own modest way."

Jane considered this a moment in silence, then said, "What did your mama say when you told her?"

"She thinks I'm very brave to shackle myself to one of Miss Prism's ladies. I shall make sure she knows you aren't responsible for my black eye."

The door opened suddenly without a warning tap. Swann stepped in, followed by Harriet. "Ah, there you are, Miss Lonsdale. Lady Pargeter seems to have disappeared. We wanted to ask her if it would be convenient for Miss Stowe to start work tomorrow morning."

"I'm sure that will be fine, Harriet," Jane said.

Her friend apologized a dozen times for taking such an abrupt departure. As Harriet apologized, Swann noticed that Fenwick was holding on to Jane's hand as if he were afraid she'd escape.

"I believe I catch a whiff of April and May," he said archly.

"Miss Lonsdale has done me the honor of accepting an offer of marriage—I think?" Fenwick said, looking a question at Jane.

Harriet looked aghast. "Jane! Are you sure? Oh, I'm sorry, milord. I don't mean to suggest—but your temper is rather—not that you didn't have a good reason to be so angry if you *love* her."

"Of course he loves her," Swann said. "Any fool can see that. Not that I mean you're a fool, Miss Stowe. How should you know? You haven't seen him sulking and skulking about like a dashed hermit when he thought I had the inner track. About them black swans, Fen—when do you figure they'll arrive?"

"You'll have to go and fetch them. I thought you'd want to see them before purchasing."

"Ah. I'll drop Fletcher a note this very night." He turned to Harriet. "Perhaps you could help me write it, Miss Stowe? I'm not much of a hand at writing. Dashed pen always splatters ink on me."

They went to the library table to write the letter. Fenwick looked at Jane. She nodded, and they both slipped quietly from the library. Instead of returning to the saloon, they went into a small parlor for privacy's sake.

"Well?" Fenwick said. "Is it a bargain, or are you going to jilt me after I've made the announcement?"

"Knowing your violent temper, I had better accept."

"Much better," he said, with a smile of infinite tenderness, and kissed her.